<<*speedfactory*>>

Player-1 <jvk20@hermes.cam.ac.uk>
John Kinsella

Player 2 <bernard@hermes.net.au>
Bernard Cohen

Player 3 <tawhite@cyllene.uwa.edu.au>
Terri-ann White

Player 4 <mw35@is6.nyu.edu>
McKenzie Wark

First published 2002 by
FREMANTLE ARTS CENTRE PRESS
25 Quarry Street, Fremantle
(PO Box 158, North Fremantle 6159)
Western Australia.
www.facp.iinet.net.au

Part of Game #1 appeared previously in *Angelaki*, vol 4, no 3.

Production Coordinator Cate Sutherland.
Cover Designer Marion Duke.
Typeset by Fremantle Arts Centre Press.
Printed by Griffin Press.

National Library of Australia
Cataloguing-in-publication data

  Speed factory.

  ISBN 1 86368 381 X.

  1. Short stories, Australian. I. Cohen, Bernard, 1963– .

  A 823.010803

The State of Western Australia has made an
investment in this project through ArtsWA in
association with the Lotteries Commission.

Contents

This book does not have a point at which it is authored, but a vector, these lines between. I email you three hundred words, then you email me three hundred words. And there is an error correction protocol: if the receiver doesn't receive within forty-eight hours after sending, the receiver sends the next three hundred words too.

Part I

John Kinsella & McKenzie Wark

Game #1

It was a strange text to be reading in flight, and yet strangely comforting. I underlined a sentence and noted the following information in the margin: Ground speed: 1,021 kilometres per hour. Altitude: 10,061 metres. Distance travelled: 373 kilometres. The time was 1.15pm, and there was still an estimated ten hours and fifteen minutes to go until we reached our destination.

And here is the sentence: 'When a plane shoots downward out of control, its crew cramp themselves fearfully into their seats for minutes like years, expecting the crash: but the smoothness of that long dive continues to their graves. Only for survivors is there an after-pain.'[1]

T E Lawrence knew of what he spoke. He had experience of speed — and died in a motorcycle crash. I imagine the telemetry Qantas put up on the screen, the numbers flickering as the plane dives, the speed rising, the altitude falling, the distance to destination stuck weirdly where it is like a vain, dishonoured promise.

But then what exactly is the promise of speed? It strikes me that Lawrence was more honest than most, in naming death itself as the imminent thing. And it strikes me that speed is only speed if there is writing. Movement is just movement, but movement that involves a dividing up of the thing moved into segments, the marking of their destination and relative position, the measurement of their progress and state — this is speed. The production of facts out of movement, and movement out of facts — this is speed.

Or this, at least, is what I write in my notebook about it, on the plane home from one side of the planet to the other, after we met and talked about writing this book together. This book about speed. Or perhaps I had intentionally forgotten that in 1896 in Indiana, when someone issued the first driver's licence, speed was subtextual. A car nearly took me out on a corner a few mornings back, and as fate would have it, it was in exactly the same place that my partner had been run over a year earlier.

It's New York, 1899 — a driver is being arrested for going twelve miles an hour. Hyperdrive. It's 1997 and a biker is using a claw hammer to prise open the door of an ex-mate who's been cooking a barrel-load of speed in his kitchen.

As he bursts in he can't help admiring the volatile liquids, the exquisite cross between the domestic and commercial that is the operation, that is the home living space.

I take stock. I scroll through my diary. I scroll. The kerning of the letter 'a' constantly introduces unwanted space in the narrative. It irritates me. It slows things down. And the false page break has a sentence hanging below it — widows and orphans, an accident on the water as the fast boat skips over a piece of barely submerged debris and deflects into nothingness. Because that's what's at the end of it — at the end of peak hour, the drama before the stock exchange closes for the day.

The rapid gesture fuses with sleep and the nightmares rush on and on and on. The faster it gets, the more it labours through the thin veins in the brain. Dilating them, interfering with the quick sparks leaping like a Forbes poem across the synaptic gap. Like the come-on of acid or strychnine. That brittle accelerating laugh. The crack up. I look to you to modulate and you are not there, where I address you. You too are volatile.

This book does not have a point at which it is authored, but a vector, these lines between. I email you three hundred words, then you email me three hundred words. And there is an error correction protocol: if the receiver doesn't receive within forty-eight hours after sending, the receiver sends the next three hundred words too. As I hammer the keyboard, I can't help admiring the transient geometry of packet switching, despatching chunks of data from one side of the planet to the other. Speed perfected.

Only, as Paul Virilio famously noted, every technology programs its own accident.[2] So I'm recording here the fact that this is what happened: I won the toss and kicked off this speed writing process, but your server crashed, you lost time, you asked for another forty-eight hours. Which reminds me of something I read in a magazine. Wait, I'll find it ... here it is: 'Last year 60 people dropped dead as they walked off planes at Heathrow airport — and it wasn't the airline food.'[3]

Economy Class Syndrome: long delays without moving your legs, blood pooling and clotting in your feet, the clots travelling to your lungs, causing a speedy death. The accident programmed by commercial jet traffic.

But is the accident always a tragedy? The book is the accident of writing. Writing is a way of dividing sense up into bits, and inscribing these bits on a surface, in order to get sense moving from one place and time to another.

All those cuneiform marks — turns out most of them were accounts of tributes to the Babylonian state. But then, the accident — the *Epic of Gilgamesh*, transcribed from speech to clay, and down through the centuries, from parchment to paper. Sense moving in slomo. But I gotta tell you, it's the waiting that kills me.

Waiting for free time. Waiting for the score. Waiting for real love. Waiting for green lights. All this time that is not itself. All this time lived in anticipation of some other time. All this time that is not itself, but exists for me only because of the possibility of a time to come.

All of lived time anticipates death. All of lived time is waiting — except when I forget that I am waiting. It's not hard to see why suicide has its own gravity, its own pull. It is just forgetting to wait. A tailspin of forgetting. I think this is why waiting brings out the worst in people. You see it every day. Drivers, caught in a jam, honking and yelling.

If every technology programs its own accident, what if every speed induces its own kind of waiting? What if, for every acceleration of speed, there was an equal and opposite wait that awaits us? Hell is the wait. But here is the strange thing — how this unnatural time, this time that exists only in anticipation of another time, can become something pure. We become junkies of the wait.

Slumped blank against time, leaning on it like a prop, the waiting body is free from any demand other than readiness for the time to come. The wait can become a permanent state, not anticipating the time of action to come, but as a parallel existence, completely detached from anticipation.

Perhaps this is the pure invention of these times. Not the invention of pure speed, but the invention of pure waiting. Waiting that anticipates nothing. Time lived without anticipation of some other kind of time, but in a serene slackness devoid of any expectation. The wait, the subtext, the static that counters any report of progress. You see, you can only guess at what it will be like once the finishing line has been crossed.

Up until that point what it's like over the crest as you put the pedal to the metal, flatline the turbo, pull the plunger back so that swirl of blood does something overtly scientific, is only conjecture. The technology of break, of entering the surface, the ups and downs of the curvature, count for nothing. An answering machine played back over and over is soothing. It slows you down. But is this what you want? You tell yourself that you're killing closure.

Speed kills, take smack instead. The catseyes form a continuous strip of light like a copy of *High Times* in the toilet. You half-flush. A minor embolism. Externally, something responds rapidly. Ah, Freedom is not merely, not merely, not merely ... disclose the essential long ungrounded, disclose exposure of being disclosed-ness, as such being *ek-sistent*, *Da-sein*, a chewing gum that buzzes the gums and has you busy busy busy, hoovering the grass like litigation.

And suddenly it's night, and you ignite existent theology. I believe I believe so rapidly muttered under your breath, waking no one, no one at all. What I want to know is what's in a brand name. What type do you use? At the eye of the cyclone is General Electric, and White knew this. They pulled up at the bottom of his driveway in the white Holden and yelled from the car— we know what you're up to! The Feds are moving in.

You hear this in every Balmain hotel that's left over from the 70s. Though some say it was a Mustang. Some, that there were four poets and a professor of English in the car, others that it was entirely empty. Truth is, truth is manner, all manner of *ek-sistence*. We know you cared, Patrick, we know the injustice of it all got to you. We — I — speed-read your oeuvre and polished it off tidily this side of eighteen hours.

Sydney Harbour vibrates as Ken Done sets up another canvas just beyond the fallout from the shells of the Opera House, the colours so — well — vibrant and ready, colours of iron, oxygen, Sydney, 'because Sydney is what I have in my blood.'[4] White had rust in the blood, residues of White cells nuked by speed.

Snapshots in a flawed lens: White in America, watching *The Wizard of Oz* while war breaks out, feeling like his novelist's vocation carried away 'by the flood of history.' White at war, Spengler and Dostoyevsky high-wiring through his head, with some more elemental White clinging to Judy Garland's technicolor rainbow 'as the Stukas flew overhead in the desert.'

White in London, where 'falling bombs and Eyre's *Journal* started in me a longing for Australia and some kind of creative urge.' A place and time of radical uncertainty, in which it was yet still possible to read at peace. White posted to HQ Fighter Command at Bentley Priory, a structure which 'concealed a ganglion of nerves which reached out through the British Isles from an underground operations room.'

White in the desert again, going through the pockets of dead airmen for letters, maps, diaries — gathering intelligence. 'Our activities were probably only of importance for the novelist in myself.' A novelist who sees in Dickens the 'intact jugular' of life that must persist, amid the detonations, at least in writing — life's other speed. White demobbed, unlearning habits of writing acquired in intelligence work, growing 'drunk cultivating a garden of words.'

But perhaps there is no Patrick White the novelist without these other Whites, the ones crouching in the shadow of immense machines, of war and cinema, of movement and information. These other Whites lived in the lees of speed, speed on an industrial scale, and dreamed of another kind of desert, where figures walk again knowing that the shadows cast across their path by the sky are just a surprise of clouds. This is Francis Webb getting his reds-under-the-bed tuppence worth, though it drifted like a cold-war haze into the decimal era, as if White had platinum fillings.

There's a subtext here, of course, and one recognises it. The whites of their eyes, the blankness of the Australian canvas that just needs to be filled, the live and let live scenario turned upside down by General Electric. Oh, that last weird sentence (something vanished — we're also getting a bit of that! which I kinda like) — I just checked the sentmail — has dropped into White's lived-in field, the lines of speed, speed on an industrial scale, a speed that makes the city of Sydney a beautiful network of roads and trees and chunks of plasterboard.

Ah, that bloody path by the sky as protests choke throats in Bankstown — they'd better not wreck our Olympics with their claims claims claims! There's a press conference held in London and Germaine Greer says don't sit there that chair is reserved for — well, for you.

This is not a problem, not a problem at all. But it's true we're having server problems and as Uni is wrapping up and students going down I'm caught in this maelstrom of work. I think the book will be brilliant and it's the big project on the horizon for me at the moment. So rest assured, within a short period of time it will be all systems go. Could ... end ... that would be great — should have read:

Not at all — I'm right into *Speed Factory*!!!! Like *Show Girls*. The film that simply everyone hated, darling. But it's true we're having server problems and as Uni is wrapping up and I'm caught in this maelstrom of work and think the book will be brilliant and it's the big project other than White on an industrial scale, and desert, where figures walk again knowing that clouds make binaries and this is all about quotas dangling over head like overheads.

Collaborative writing is like sex. Attempting to match speeds between bodies. Technical difficulties. Can't get the condom on or that bit of clothing off. My server is down; my libido, crashed. Same antimony of anxiety: why does the other not respond to this movement? Or else: what does the other's response to this movement mean? Perhaps the only difference is that it's possible still to live with the illusion that sex is not caught up in some vast machinery of speeds, whereas literature is obviously factory work. Its deadlines, pub dates — movement on the industrial scale.

I reckon the subtext to HIV-AIDS hysteria is the recognition that sex is not private. Like writing, it's connected, in this case to a huge medical and legal apparatus, to contraceptive technology, abortion rights, age of consent law reform. Wherever there is speed, there is the virus of technical difficulties.

Ken Slessor, official war correspondent, poet of speed, struggling to rendezvous in England with Noela, his love, and get a dispatch past the censors back to the folks in Australia. But it's high time to ask: do women experience speed differently? Slessor writes women out of the beginning of the story when he describes leaving Sydney on a massive troop convoy in 1940:

'There were women on the other side of Sydney Cove, standing there dumbly in the drifts of rain, clinging to the wet iron and staring through the railings with a hungry intentness. They made no effort to wave. Their faces, white and strained and tiny in the distance, hardly moved. All through the morning I noticed them and was aware of their thin hands gripping the iron, and the rain over their knuckles and running over their wedding rings.'[5]

Women's bodies barred from nautical vectors but no longer Lords, where it raineth in the long room and the pavilions spill saffron over the East India Company, and good ol' Josh stalks Rebecca. Ah, tastes good. Mr Speed says it's a crying shame that Warney soiled his good name like that and comes out with someone else's line — 'we are dangerous', I know, one thing being letteral and the other liter-al, we ARE at war; concurrently, the roman rack and foot clamps and oligarchy that is cricket has them snaring good wickets like deferred pain, desiring always the postscript — that stat rather than the score, undermining team spirit as with the Great Australian Novel which must be a quick but long read that drags you through all manner of terrains.

The long and straight of it is Roman on the M roads, even country lanes sprouting again like coppice or subspace signatures beneath the carapace, the canals throwing up their stuff and the inquisitors measuring a body for chains and cage, wedging the foot, inciting cameras as the fines will go straight into the police's coffers, and *The Boys* is a hit in a few London cinemas — the praise is lavish and everything is true grit and good.

The bookie makes a quick buck. A killing. A packet. An English commentator calls the atmosphere 'festive'. Long wave, medium wave, short wave. Like haircuts and other cultural baggage stuck in a warehouse down by the waterfront. A dumb lawyer races towards his client in a clapped-out Pontiac. Chromed pipeware tables and chair, packed full of gear, tremble in anticipation of free houses, flex under the weight of dusty old paperbacks. Penguins, mostly. Old wartime Penguins from the 40s in regulation orange jackets. Literary modernism gone to war in servicemen's pockets. Penguin Modern Classics from the 70s in Germano Facetti covers, a Dali painting gracing the cover of Sartre's *Nausea*, as if the two were interchangeable. Penguin Twentieth Century Classics from the 90s, fronted mostly by nostalgic black and white photographs of a modern world well lost.

These books built empires of literary speed from the Outer Hebrides to the New Hebrides. Modern content packaged in modern form. I pick one up and read it. I become Virginia Woolf, driving, writing, rapturing the evening's shapes and colours in a Sussex landscape, 'overcome by beauty extravagantly greater that one could expect … I cannot hold this — I cannot express this — I am overcome by it — I am mastered.'[6]

But not completely, out from under this mastered self appear another, that resists, that insists that self is mastery itself. Selves dispute: To master or be mastered by beauty? A third self appears and places the line of cliffs firmly in the past. 'I feel life left behind even as the road is left behind.' Then a fourth self, like an intermittent signal: 'I feel suddenly attached, not to the past but to the future. I think of Sussex in five hundred years to come.'

Out of this fissure of selves, Woolf smooths out a slipstream of an idea: 'Look, I will make a little figure for your satisfaction; here he comes. Does this little figure advancing through beauty, through death, to the economical, powerful and efficient future ... satisfy you?' A rattle of Virginias cry 'Yes! Yes!' But then another voice airs something different: 'Eggs and bacon; toast and tea; fire and bath'. The body comes to stump these flights of mind.

Comes unread as fiscal policy dictates the arts council strikes deep into the bunkers, pinpoint and stealthlike the Penguin 60s classics version of Jean-Jacques Rousseau's *Meditations Of A Solitary Walker* has me walking as the Butcher of Baghdad amongst the many hearts of Richard Burton and date palms, the three wise men in my daughter's nativity play Tony Blair, Bill Clinton, and maybe the French President, or was that wishful thinking? He defers and condemns and makes a pact with Russia. World opinion trembles and grows solid, again.

I am Jean-Jacques saying print will map my virtual digressions: But I was still counting on the future, and I hoped that a better generation, examining more closely both the judgement pronounced against me by the present generation and its conduct towards me towards me towards me towards me, would find it easy to unravel the stratagems of those who control it and would at last see me as I really am. They laugh at Tony Benn who says in parliament — you' re all immoral.

Headsets on and the B52s rock on. As Thoreau is prompted out of the leather bindings on State occasions, impeached over and over and over: They mistake who assert that the Yankee has few amusements because he has not so many public holidays ... the decor riddled green with envy on the opposition's mug shots, war makes a prime minister memorable, the new generation cruise missiles actually being cheaper and more accurate, and tornadoes comin' in fast once the AA is muted, them's our boys, oh war reporter, Slessor, Virginia Woolf eating asparagus. Eating feminism as if it mattered. The dust the dust and CNN hanging in there, decked up on the ministry of information, barely weighed down by flak jackets and the *son et lumière:*

Thursday is the net for weddings in Iraq, they've grown used to it and know the wisdom (pearl of the other orient) behind the twenty-year-old's words in the London *Evening Standard*: 'It can't be helped when civilians get in the way', How blind that cannot see serenity!' How blind that cannot see serenity How blind that cannot see serenity — yet strangely comforting. Particularly the details. Paul Beaver, group spokesman for *Jane's Defence*, says in the papers that twelve Tornado strike aircraft launched attacks with Paveway III laser-guided bombs, which are strengthened to penetrate concrete bunkers. Accurate to about three metres, they are almost as good as

Tomahawk cruise missiles, which are accurate to two metres. Tomahawks cost ten times more than Paveways. Never mind the quality feel the width, as the South London spiv says as he slips the bolt back into the car boot.

But wait! There's more! The bombs dropped on Baghdad in 1998 are 'four times' more accurate than in 1991. So they say. We'll have to wait and see. The only point to the bombing is to get the arms inspectors back into Iraq — to assess how effective the technology was. 'After all, somebody has to check on the damage caused to the weapons of mass destruction. That is the only possible endgame from the latest round of military operations.'[7] Get those post-Patrick White airforce intelligence types back in to measure how much progress we're making. Poets of the vector, of novel telemetries. War as the production of ever more precise facts. As Bertold Brecht already knew, 'strategy has turned into surgery'.[8] Saddam Hussein's last card — make the West wait for its test results. I keep buying the morning and evening editions, but the result is always a draw.

Brecht again: 'The spectator's need ... to be distracted from his daily warfare is continually reproduced by that daily warfare, but is just as continually in conflict with his need to be able to control his own fate.' And so I wait, and anticipate. Hovering and hoovering, a back and forth rhythm; the push of desire, the pull of anxiety. A nervous system of appliances, a network of servers.

On the way from Sydney to New York, I'm at LAX airport in Los Angeles the day before Xmas. Somebody left an unattended bag in the American Airlines terminal. The bomb squad mobilises against this unknown, and we passengers wait while the space is cordoned. Meanwhile, everything proceeds as normal in the Delta terminal next door. As if a potential bomb in the American terminal would not rip through the wall into the space of a rival airline. The bomb routine has become so much a part of everyday life that these absurdities are barely noticeable. The potential dangers of a space must be contained within limits, even if nobody knows what those limits should be.

Nobody knows when an airport or a country is really free from weapons of mass destruction. But it is important to produce the appearance of producing facts about dangers. Weapons inspectors, bomb disposal teams, fact finding missions, international observers, criminal psychiatrists, royal commissions, the grand jury, investigative journalism, smoke detectors — the telemetry of everyday life, signals mapping the threat and thread of unpredictable movements. I log on to check the weather over Sydney, over Bagdhad. I search the hard disc for a note I think I filed somewhere.

Here it is. Kathy Acker writes: 'How can we, as Hannah Arendt says, even in worlds that seem to have become inhuman, remain obligated to these worlds? Obligated, for being writers, our job is to hear and put together narrations and so give meaning to what seems to be or is inhuman.'[9] How can we, even inside the speed factory, write in the name of a more democratic time, a more civil space? Maybe I'm just depressed by the knowledge, brought to light in a Pakistani court, that even cricket becomes corrupted. Alternatively, the corrupt make the best captains. And after all, it — winning, that is — is only relative. A long break, a leg break, express bowling.

I pause and take stock. An age. I've collected a stack of footnotes and am tracking down the primary text at the moment. An experiment with time. The rush as Marina Warner's *Joan of Arc* enters my mind's eye — it's so visual: On two counts, Joan grievously flouted the laws of Chivalry, thus endangering herself in a world that still paid lip-service and bringing about part of her condemnation.[10] Object, ego, signifier. Prayer is instant — measured outside time. It can't even be compared to something fast — say like the speed of light. There's no 'relatively speaking'. Damnation comes in an instant, maybe the instant it's repealed. Grace and Damnation are simultaneous, ever present. Like Monsanto releasing genetically modified rape seed into the environment. They'll plead guilty. It pays to.

The *Book of Margery Kempe*: 'Nevertheless, daughter, I have ordained you to be a mirror amongst them, to have great sorrow, so that they should take example from you to have some little sorrow in their hearts for their sins, so that they might through that be saved; yet they have no love to hear of sorrow or of contrition.'[11] Finite. Limiting? Mass and body. Discrete variables as the analogue turns on the table. There's a child with a paper cone with a pin stuck through the tapered end. Black Sabbath crackles. A Led Zeppelin record is compelled backwards.

There's rapture in this, if you know the subtext. It might be a poem by a famous Australian poet. His rise was, well, almost rapid. The snow has been and gone. Deep below the surface of the fens the peat smoulders. At Wicken they clear the scrub so the nouns can grow incrementally. A certain kind of bumble bee will prosper amongst their determined stance. From the old tower hide we watch a variety of waterbirds settle. There are rumours of otters, tracking from watercourse to watercourse, across the fens. Nearby, the Bishop of Ely counts the collection and thinks about Maundy Money.

Have just been chatting with Tom Pynchon, but I don't use mobile telephones ... wait a minute, there's someone on the other line. Sorry wrong number. Your call has been placed in a queue, and will be answered by the first available sales representative. While global capital accelerates to light speed, King of the optical fibre, consumer sovereignty waits in line. But does any speed make any sense any more without an absolute speed, against which to experience its limits, its finitude?

In Carl Dreyer's film, *The Passion of Joan of Arc*, Joan (Maria Falconetti) stares, not at the camera, but through it, staring through light, air, celluloid, staring through retina, memory, burning into timelessness. Joan is not waiting for kangaroo court justice. She stares through us to another time. Only Antonin Artaud, in a now famous bit part, stares at Jean the way Jean stares at time. There is something inhuman about it.

If for Hannah Arendt, the problem is one of maintaining a human communication within the inhuman world of the speed factory, for Dreyer the problem is something else again. The speed factory interfaces with us via the image of the face — it graces every screen and magazine and record cover. These faces are prosthetic extensions of the inhuman into the human world. I have no idea how a TV or a CD works, but faces smile from both, real friendly, beckoning me.

But Dreyer makes the face that stares from the speed factory's most prestigious screen, its silver screen, one that stares into another kind of inhuman world, one not of our making. Dreyer's Joan stares out from the merely human death sentenced by the courts, and stares through to absolute death. Dreyer found a way to orient the machinery of speed, the cinematic apparatus, the grinding gears of relative speeds, to something outside their merely relative gains and waits.

Not every machine works so effectively. Dreyer's own apparatus didn't always run smooth. Or think of the legal apparatus that consigned Joan to the flames. It didn't intend thereby to make her immortal, a precocious celebrity.

One thing we didn't take into account when starting *Speed*

Factory — it would not just be an account of the accident, it would itself be prey to accidents, and this would slow it down. It was not, fortunately, a textual machine of much efficiency. What I propose is to end part one with these three hundred words. As Cioran says, 'a book should be a danger' — the writing as much as the reading of it.[12]

Danger puts form at risk of deformation. To give form, to inform, requires also an element of deforming. Information is pattern with a hole in it. The paradox of the speed factory: the disorder that premises its orderings. What I now fear is writing made safe, and thereby made to serve. Writing gets pressed into service, becomes a manufacturing, not a manufracturing. 'In times of war … the doctrine of "national service" gains enormous force, which can be turned to the establishing, for peacetime, of a corresponding doctrine of service to the community.'[13] Which is what 'literature' has become, service to the moral order of the state — its textual line of defence, security.

As John Anderson wrote in the 40s: '… servility is rapidly gaining ground. The process has, of course, been greatly accelerated by the war; this might, indeed, if we abstract from particular national aims and consider the whole society of predatory nations, be described as the "purpose" of the war. Naive persons believe, because one side is opposed to freedom, that the other side must be in favour of it.' A thought worth reviving in the cruise missile age.

Bernard Cohen & McKenzie Wark

Game #2

Despite our APEX expectations of Paris, the destination marker sits squarely over London. We passengers stare at the video projection screen, willing the plane to change course, to fly towards the indicated landing point instead of along this unpredicted hypotenuse. We are veterans of too many airport movies and too many video games, and there is a ridiculous terror in the GAME OVER outcome which must follow this. The seemingly mis-aimed icon follows its passage between the warzones: Da Nang, Kabul, Baghdad, Kharkov. These are the recognisable names between Bali and Athens.

An announcement: the pilot assures us we are not flying to London: Paris is a new route, and Zero Point Paris has yet to be programmed into the system. Hmmmn. It could be me alone, but I imagine row after row of tightened, doubting lips. Our symbol sits still on the screen, or jerks forward pixel by pixel.

As we get closer to northern France, the skew path becomes more disturbing; I am more disturbed by it. Despite the pilot's soothing techno-talk and, on-screen, battle markers superseded by wine-producing centres and punctuated by the periodic stillness of the airline logo, all purity (the round-ended metal tube, evenly spaced passengers struggling for sleep positions, weighed meal portions on rectangular trays, flight attendants' perfectly practised routines) is gone, muddied by this minor techno-gap. We descend, the altitude measure dropping at near enough to 10m/s, the distance from destination almost unaltered. Switch it off! I brace as the altitude falls below three hundred metres. I'm gripping the armrests, pushing myself back against the upright seat, telling myself: come on, relax, relax, it's routine. The screen eventually goes blank. And as usual I'm thinking about farewell notes, who should be mentioned.

Some books it's best not to read as inflight entertainment. 'I don't know what to call this story', Marguerite Duras writes.[14] The story of a young British pilot, shot down near the village of Vauville, in the last days of the war. 'The child remained a prisoner of his airplane.' And Duras becomes a prisoner of death, through this death. The whole village did. The women tend his grave still. 'Death baptizes as well.' It brings into community this 'child who had died from playing at war, from playing at being the wind.'

Duras writes, again and again, around this fact of death. 'It's a brutal, isolated fact, without reverberation', an 'inexhaustible fact'. And perhaps this is one way for writing to find another speed, a speed outside the machinery of war and commerce. But how? 'There is nothing I can write. There should be a writing of non-writing. Someday it will come ... Lost. Written, there. And immediately left behind.'

Women's experience: the body rubbed against a particular speed. Her body labouring, making and being made by the house, making the house a home, a factory of domestic speed. 'A house means a family house, a place specially meant for putting children and men in so as to restrict their waywardness and distract them from the longing for adventure and escape they've had since time began.'[15]

Men and children fly off, caught in other factories, other speeds — school, work, war. 'I can recall the kind of silence there was after they went out. To enter that silence was like entering the sea.' A deep sea. 'There'd been nine generations of women before me within those walls ... All over the house there were surfaces rubbed smooth where grown-ups, children, and dogs had gone in and out of the doors.'

The plane lands smoothly enough, at 246 kilometres per hour or thereabouts, and fluent as a game of tennis — 'thock, thock' as Tranter would (has) put it[16] — wheels bouncing moderately for a few metres, the force of airbrakes which all pilots no doubt wish for, and the only cure for my tremendous vertigo is to be flat on my face (flat against someone else's face is actually better, though it risks a vertigo of intimacy which is also a form of compulsive jumping); momentary ignorance is no help, not with my experience.

At the hotel I pull Barthelme's *City Life* from my travel bag. I'm feeling blokey, in need of undermining. I re-read the story beginning 'A dog jumped on me out of a high window.' The story's called 'The Falling Dog'.[17] I suppose it's about inverse vertigo, the fear of being jumped upon. There's no analysis of speed, and I'm in the mood for empirics. I suppose it's a stupid story, but 'good-stupid', like his 'stupid' story about capitalism which does manage to contain a critique of capital's logic. And it takes my mind off falling as a death-act, which I hope means I will fall asleep. The dog falls three or four stories before landing on the protagonist. Barthelme breaks into verse:

'I looked at the dog. He looked at me.
who else has done dogs? Baskin, Bacon, Landseer,
    Hogerth, Hals
with leashes trailing as they fall
with dog impedimenta following: bowl, bone, collar,
    licence, Gro-pup.'

It's a sick tactic, to soothe myself with the falling dogs of literature. I'm coming to hate gravity, for all its organisational ability. How do solitons — models for the new message factories — manage to resist its effect for mile after mile at constant speed? Do dogs fall, or do they jump? I fall asleep without figuring it out. Or do I jump to sleep? It's all so difficult, words. Dreaming of jumping cats. On waking, crumpled on the bed, I remember this jumping cat thing comes from something I read in [Newspaper] once.[18] The record for falling cats in New York is thirty-four storeys. The cat suffered a broken leg, but lived. Some New York cat hospital keeps score.

Cats have a lower terminal velocity than humans. It's funny how you fall faster and faster, then you just fall at the same speed. Then you bounce. Cats bounce well, apparently, and fall slowly. Their fur adds wind resistance. Humans fall head first, air slipstreaming around the cranium.

I always imagined cats and dogs are things that might jump or have a fall. But what if it's all the other way around? What if jumping or falling is something that might have a cat, or a dog, or a person? What if I don't sleep, but am sleeped? What if I don't dream, but become dreamt? Why do we think, because we are a noun, that we have verbs? What if verbs have us? What if there are only verbs? No, no, that's not right. What if there is only verbing. No, still not … Whating becoming verbing. Verbing becoming whating. Becoming verbing whating. Yes …

Fire up the laptop, plug the modem into the nearest phone socket. There's email from you. Something for

Speed Factory, finally, and an apology: 'My computer's gone down, so I realise this may be out of time. If so, sorry about that, and just leave it out.' So I email you back: 'The rules of this game are flexible. Speed bent like light around humans, humans bent like water around speed.'

Meaning, I think: email is a rotten medium for complaint, a channel in which jokes must be explained, curtness is the way of life, everything subtle draws in a tendency to insult. Perhaps the problem is that email has not yet in place a natural-feeling phatic system. To compensate, a profusion of winks and friendship indicators, explanations, over-articulated apologia. You reply with clarity rather than literature. That's your re-assurance: it's a game, it's okay, it's fun, relax. Later, though, you display another attitude: I see your vision of the speed factory's nature of manufacture. You envisage the transformation of mundane communications into poetry.

(I could remain polite, and write 'the poetic', but that's hardly an alchemical term and, anyway) I'm still sitting back when your speed factory product arrives: I'm unpoetic, 'receiving'. I am still mannered by the medium, as though only an email has arrived, rather than writing from a writer. (The dogs and cats fall away; gravity's negligible action on waves in canals is outside the scope; terminal velocities are reconfigured to refer to the speed of plugging in.) I like your abstractions, speed subject to quantum mechanics in relation to the human; speed solidified, humans flexible. But I am not convinced by your means of arrival (I'm still worried about email, maybe, or maybe I'm a closet Cartesian). Fiona Capp's dog falls asleep under the table of a Paris jazz bar: not far to tumble, not even for an Alsatian. The dog sleeps through the seduction scene: 'Eva rested her head on Marcel's shoulder, her black, shining bob curling around her ears. His hand hovered at the base of her back.'[19]

So Capp sleeps the dog, sleeps together her characters. And my insecure ego-sense cannot accept that I am breathed by the Melbourne air. Although the Melbourne air, no doubt, respires sleeping dogs, and cats, and humans, without too much fret.

Perhaps it's just that even though my laptop has been in my life for some time, it hasn't yet passed into the writing. Computers, networks — tools for writing, but not yet belonging to writing, and though writing, belonging to life.

Georges Perec knew about this. 'The passage of time (my history) leaves behind a residue that accumulates: photographs, drawings, the corpses of long since dried up felt pens ... this is what I call my fortune.'[20] And my fortune, if I think about it, includes discarded computers, dusty boxes of old computer discs, email archives in obsolete formats. Now that they are old, worn, scarred with the accidents of life, these effusions of the speed factory can become part of the everyday, and through the everyday, part of literature.

I know when Perec's writing became part of me. I wrote it in the margin: 'Read on flight QF 17 taking off from LAX in 26th July, 1998.' And these are the lines I wrote that beside: 'Reading isn't merely to read a text, to decipher signs, to survey lines, to explore pages, to traverse a meaning; it isn't merely the abstract communion between author and reader, the mystical marriage between the Idea and the ear. It is, at the same time, the noise of the Métro, or the swaying of a railway compartment, or the heat of the sun on a beach and the shouts of the children playing a little way off, or the sensation of hot water in the bath, or the waiting for sleep.'

Isn't it just the feeling of familiarity about the places within which the book is read that makes the phatic dimension of books seem so agreeably friendly?

'A work consisting of refused communications.'[21] It was Elias Canetti's idea, only I think perhaps we're writing it.

I learn so much from Canetti, above all from his refusal of good form, the smashed language, broken down to catch the speed of thought.

'A "modern" man has nothing to add to modernism, if only because he has nothing to oppose it with. The well-adapted drop off the dead limb of time like lice.'

Isn't that why some of us became postmodernists? Only time caught us up again. Few from our pod will be sharp enough to cut through time.

'A shattering thought: there may be nothing to know, and error comes only because we try to know it.'

Now there you have it — the thought from the outside. But did anyone else ever put it so pointedly? Canetti's though is alway sharp, but he points the tip away.

I keep a collection of Canetti quotes on file in this laptop. I forget when or where I first read him. I forget when I keyed in the passages I'd marked. I even forget if it was this computer, or an older one, from which the whole file might have subsequently been ported. In any case, there's a duplicate file, including the Canetti, on my other computer, in the office.

Circa 2000: These quotations go with me everywhere. Some Canetti, Woolf, lots of Montaigne. They make home for me — especially some selected words by friends. There's even some of you in there. And I carry this with me, from Alberto Manguel:

Circa 1000: 'To avoid parting with his collection of 117,000 books while travelling, the avid reader and Grand Vizier of Persia, Abdul Kassem Ismael, has them carried by a caravan of four hundred camels, trained to walk in alphabetical order.'[22]

Mm, which goes to show how out the rate of the folding up of language has accelerated: a carry rate of fewer than three hundred books per beast would hardly be worth boasting about today. I picture them snaking along the crests of the dunes.

'Deviation without sweetness is corrupt,' claims the proverb generator I've installed in my laptop (the generator I suspect was responsible for the previous crash of my desktop computer, a crash which separated 850 word files from their names and creation dates, exposed the lack of orderliness in which I work, the impropriety of my drafting practices, meant that instead of being up to a definable point with pieces of writing I was comparing three or four similar drafts and unable to choose between them). 'Sobriety is like a Nashville geisha,' it says also.

My remnant feeling is that work remains precarious, and this is emphasised not only by the down state of my desktop computer now (bus problem, according to it) but metonymised in the current state of the bookshelf to my left (which I banged together last year from a couple of old kitchen shelves). The shelf is leaning sharply to the left, held up only by the proximate bench. It's quite a good design really, or idea for a design ('quite a good accident' would be more precise), the shelf as image of inability to bear. It has only ninety-four books (plus a few pamphlets), all paperbacks except *Lenin: Selected Works*; *Journey to Armenia* by Osip Mandelstam; and David Dietz's 1945 pop-sci number, *Atomic Energy in the Coming Era* (coverline: 'The Great New Bomb …')

Skipping through my sources I find an epigraph for the Menzies book. I almost know I'm back into the writing.

(And as HackProverbs momentarily insists, 'knowledge ratifies itself.') In the process of moving my library out of the apartment, I found a bit of duralex glass behind the couch. The books just took over the place, like in Canetti's *Auto Da Fe*. Either they go or I go. Books have such a physical presence. The little buggers just quietly digest themselves, the acid in the paper ruminating away. And books are such indolent things. Most of the time they do nothing, just sit around, keeping their thoughts to themselves. There's something amusing about the way we all labour away to make them, and then they sit around doing fuck-all until they rot.

It's like books are the superannuation program for thoughts and feelings. If they don't get sweated out in the editing, then they're set until the end of their papery days. Anyway, this bead of duralex glass — it reminds me of the first time I 'lost' my writing on the computer. The hard disc died and took all my words with it. Of course I hadn't backed them up. It was my first computer with a hard disc and I hadn't yet learned of their alarming propensity to suicide.

Speechless with rage, I had to do something. Not just because of the loss — I'd lost notebooks before and cursed my absent mindedness — this was something more than loss. So I took out my duralex glasses, those unbreakable ones that lattés come in, and threw them at the wall, really hard, one by one. Sometimes they bounced, and I had to try again. There was a really satisfying effect when they popped. Ordinary glass can break a little, or a lot. That duralex stuff either bounces, or shatters instantly into tiny cubes. They became the tangible analogue for my lost electrons, lying doggo on their dysfuctional disc.

When I was beginning to write, I thought (liked to think) that once the words were out there, they could never be recanted ('out there' included in my notebook). I was living with abstract painters, surrounded by vastly expressive black and red canvasses. This idea of the perfection of the expressed was liberating in a kind of religious way: revelatory, practical outcomes, granting knowledge of what one must do. My subsequent liberation was in the slower embeliefment that the writer is a hitchhiker along the vectors of culture. I haven't been writing for very long; I changed from one system of self-regard to the other not that long ago.

I'm wondering what word or proto-word your duralex fragment stood in for — whether the metamorphic process from loss-beyond-loss (which I take to mean the double loss of object and faith) through the wonderful and shattering control/loss of control act through to finding that (after ten years, at a guess) the shard retained its meaningfulness as a kind of re-enchanted souvenir of your disenchantment, whether this process wiped out verbal particularity.

Perhaps this fragment is the word 'compulsion'. Did you keep it? I can accept that we are living in this exchange the refusal of communication (this you said more than a thousand words ago, and I was in a bad mood then and am varying from moment to moment now). I mistreat my sources (you are a source). I looked up Canetti in Deleuze and Guattari's *A Thousand Plateaus* and found the word 'enantiomorphosis', meaning (according to the translator) 'prohibitions on transformation'. My impulse is to note that we are writing 'Metamorphoses'. We may be refusing communication (you are a source) yet are corresponding in other ways. Eg, my Menzies epigraph was from Ovid's *Metamorphoses*.

Following behind in my car, I lost sight of the truck on the first turn. My whole library was in that truck. I thought briefly of the possibility of losing the lot. Found it strangely comforting.

Because I got there late, the removalist refused to carry the big boxes of books up the stairs. He had another job to do. Not a moving job. I heard him conspire about something on his mobile. So I had to lug the whole lot up stairs myself. I still feel the pain of it in the tendons of my left hand.

It's from pain that we learn. Or so I've learned. That there is no such thing as the text, and hence no point to interpretation; that was today's burden. Texts are weightless; books are really fucking heavy. Books are not texts, but vectors. You don't interpret them, you move, or are moved by them. As I was moved, by this impossible responsibility of owning a library.

There's nothing to it — becoming a writer — just the metamorphosis. That's it. A transformation without content, purpose, subject, goals. Other than sneaking around the traps — of authorial vanity, truck and barter. Just as there's nothing to reading, besides avoiding the trap of being in custody of a library.

There's nothing hiding in that word, 'expression', except the secret that there is nothing hiding in it. What is expressed just is. It's different from what expressed it, and from what it expresses, but in no particular or significant way. There's nothing repressed in it, just things refused.

There's no going back. No going behind the back of the text to the author, but no going back to context, discourse, the unconscious. There's only a going forward, a fresh expression. How stubbornly literature avoids this concept of itself!

Yes! I have had numerous literary experiences with removalists: 'What's in all these boxes?' one asked in 1993. (This was a move around the side of a house and into storage in a neck-high cellar. I'm with you on pain, also.)
'Books.'
'Books! No wonder they're so fucking heavy. The only reading material at my place is *Rugby League Week*, and I throw it away as soon as I'm done with it.'

And I like how easily 'fucking' and 'heavy' go together: as though books should be as light as the abstractions inside.

More literature going forward — I love it — going forward by truck, and only by you or me following these books in a car do they metamorphose into texts. (This is not the tree falls in a forest tale; the making of a book into a text is a very particular move: hence the 'you or me'. We are the ones who think in this specific transformative manner. I read a bad sci-fi book about creatures of certain molecular densities who lived in a mine and could walk through walls and were somehow [can't remember how] a danger and in the end could be destroyed by fire, and I suspect that we talk in this other dimension, at least judging from the way people try to talk to me about my writing sometimes.)

This is a reactive sort of response, I guess: my hard drive is being low-level formatted as I write (was and is a dud, a reason to abandon Macintosh), and you're wondering about disappearing libraries, and I'm thinking of packing mine into boxes again and putting it into a cellar (again) leaving it all there for six months of floods and fungus and termites.

I took my time being someone-who-writes. Or maybe time took me there, to someone-who-writes. Willing the plane to change course doesn't change it's course. It's a dumb tactic, reversing the poles, but maybe it's where the meta meets the morph.

There's nothing inside the text. Beckett led me to this (or rather hearing someone I was just getting to know and just starting to love read Beckett's poem 'Cascando' aloud to an empty kitchen, on hearing the news that someone once loved was now dead, but that's another story) and now I'm stuck with it.

God isn't dead, he's sleeping. Sleeping in the text, in the culture of text — the reverence with which readers turn pages like prayer wheels, line their walls with booky shrines, congregate at writer's festivals for that old timey revival feeling.

Writing has to be something more than work, work, work, this march of fingers and keys. Or maybe something less, something like play, like dancing. To be against the book but in favour of writing, and maybe for books that are incitements to writing, morphs that court meta.

Literature says: 'Don't fuck with me!'
Writing says: 'Fuck with me ...'

Or so I imagine, but I'm still hearing spirits, murmuring in the sleep of text. But these days books seem like brute material facts compared to 'real life'. 'Real life', where our money circles the globe, checking in and out of investment opportunities with all the patience of an electron. One second it's a high-yield government bond for Argentina, the next minute it's a bit Japanese pension fund.

But then it's not just capital that cruises, looking for the money shot, nor do laser-guided smart bombs have a monopoly on speed. So do does chat, and gossip, and rumour, all of which now have instant global means of arrival.

Jesus Fucking Christ. And toothache! Whoever said writing has no shamanistic value (this I know wasn't you!) is herewith and forthwith banished from my mind. Let it be magical, let it be healing, let it overflow with fucking hippy therapeutic value.

Come on then, writing, tell me your manifold prescriptions for pain. How do you deal with the reference of pain along the lower jaw? (When my friend had a fit, my only knowledge came from the film *One Flew Over the Cuckoo's Nest*: should I try to shove a book in there to prevent him biting off his tongue? Would his teeth fall out when his jaw slackened?) Writing, how do you deal with pain referred down the windpipe? Or the direct pain of swallowing, and added to it a burning sensation from clove oil? What about this: I think I can feel the enamel, the cubic space of the tooth, the conic root. Writing, what do you say when pain escapes from nerves, those weighty and direct organic vectors, and spends the night chasing itself into and around body space? Do something, for God's sake!

Do it, you writing, bury my mouth in your soft wet text; let me feel the seep of the most aesthetic anaesthesia. Writing, read me with reverence! Ooh, yes, that's the spot, right at the back there. Ease me, please, release me. Writing, if you are a march of fingers (oh! where is postmodern English's subjunctive when I need it?), be the march of soothing fingers; if you are work, be the work of play; if you are play, be the play of morphine on consciousness; if you are dancing, then, sure, dance, dance, but let the music be loud, the lights bright, the company distracting. And, yes, writing, fuck with me too.

Dear Sir/Madam,
I am writing on behalf of the Customer Service department of Muse Corporation in regard to the letter we received from you on 12-04-99. It is our company policy to reply promptly and courteously to all such inquiries to try and ensure that our customers are comfortable with our products.

Unfortunately, I regret to inform you that your complaints about our Writing line of products refer to features that are not available from the products offered at that particular price point. If you examine the warranty documents supplied with your copy of Writing you will find that the guarantee for that particular product does not cover situations of extreme sensation, such as pain and joy. Since you have purchased the family pack from our economy line, the inscription of sexual joy is specifically prohibited, as are expressions of physical pain deemed likely to cause alarm or discomfort to minors.

Here at Muse Corporation we aim to answer all the creative needs of our customers. I am happy to inform you that, should you wish to purchase an upgrade to improve the intensity of performance of your Writing, I can offer you a special discount on any of our premium lines.

May I draw your attention to our Intensity ValuPak product. This popular accessory will enable you to write effective and original sentences on a wide range of emotionally and physically intense topics. It covers all kinds of physical pain, and with our new surgical weapons, this release is specially useful for postmodern warfare applications.

The Intensity ValuPak can also be configured for a wide range of Writing on adult themes, including sexual joy, anxiety and dancing. You must include proof of age with your purchase order if you wish to purchase this version of Writing.

Fortunately, at that moment a dentist intervened. For $109 she vaporised both a flap of gum (my mouth is filled with the flavour of singed flesh) and sexual fantasies regarding pale models in *Harper's Bazaar*, September 1998, not that they (the fantasies and the depicted application of orange eyeliner) were particularly 'creative'.

I was squinting into the dental lamp. She asked me if I'd like to wear sunglasses: she had a pair for that very purpose.

No thanks, I said. I'll use my eyelids.

She laughed and made a series of jokes at an equivalent

level, and I laughed too, with the lignocaine needle stretching the insertion point. Would you like to spit out?

What is the difference between a patient and a customer? I might have asked, but by that time my mouth was full of surgical instruments.

I gave over that I was nervous of dentists. She wanted to know if I'd met any particularly interventionist ones and I described the ligation of a tooth lying horizontally in the roof of my mouth. She indicated that this procedure must have been conducted by the dental equivalent of a revhead. I thought the lignocaine had numbed everything, but I flinched when she jabbed so she gave me another shot. My tongue felt like someone else's, family dentist or not.

Did I wear a pacemaker, she wanted to know (routine question, of course: I don't look like a pacemaker wearer, even though I was in Leura, home of the 'Pacemaker Olympics' according to last week's *Blue Mountains Gazette*). The gum vaporiser tended to interfere with the CD player, but unfortunately the sad old soundtrack to Ally McBeal continued. What's the difference between a listener (reader, even) and a customer? I might have asked, but it would have sounded like 'woshadishersh'.

'The bourgeoisie cannot exist without constantly revolutionising the instruments of production, and thereby the relations of production, and with them the whole relations of society. Conservation of the old modes of production in unaltered form, was, on the contrary the first condition of existence for all earlier ... classes. Constant revolutionising of production, uninterrupted disturbance of all social conditions, everlasting uncertainty and agitation distinguish the bourgeois epoch from all earlier ones. All fixed fast frozen relations, with their train of ancient and venerable prejudices and opinions, are swept away. All new formed ones become antiquated before they can ossify. All that is solid melts into air, all that is sacred is profaned, and man is at last compelled to face with sober sense, his real conditions of life and relations of his kind ...'[23]

There are times when I feel that the best argument in favour of modernity, capitalism, industrialisation, the whole shebang — is dentistry. I mean it just doesn't bear thinking about, what people had to go through before modern dentistry.

Tree-hugging hippies go on about herbal medicine, and champion venerable superstitions from some ancient third world country or other where everybody dies from gastroenteritis. And hell, who knows? Maybe they got a point. Maybe putting string through your nose and drinking your own piss really is good for you. But have you ever heard of herbal dentistry?

Even Balmain's basket weavers, hell, even people in the Blue Mountains, have been known to cancel yoga class to go have a wisdom tooth extracted by a stainless-steel professional in a white coat and what by electric chair standards is one mighty comfy electric chair. Gimme that everlasting uncertainty, Karl my man, so long as I when I get this molar plugged I get the injection. Step on the gas now!

Has Karl passed the baton to the wrong man? The radio man steps on the gas. He talks about the gas, he gasbags. He likes gas. He likes electric chairs. He doesn't mind lethal injections. He understands the guillotine. He knows about gallows. He hates yoga. He is reasonable and he has strong opinions and he's convinced that these two characteristics are compatible. 'I had my teeth cleaned recently. Some of you are trying to wonder how that relates to the caning in Singapore and some of you know immediately how it relates ... I'm convinced that part of our confusion about the problem of evil in general is due to our American view of the incompatibility of love and pain.'[24]

He turns on the television.

'Marcia gets a crush on her new dentist in Paramount Television's *The Brady Bunch*. Dr. Vogel, the new family dentist, is the subject of Marcia's daydreams after she meets him. She believes that her feeling is returned when she misinterprets his interest in her as a babysitter.'[25]

We love our dentists, we love our babysitters. We feel the need for oral hygiene; we understand about parental abandonment.

I'm getting the big wind-up now from the producer. Remember, kiddies, babysitters are for loving. Dentists are for hugging. Orthodontic nurses lean across, mmm, but then there's a sharp jab in the back of the hand and count to ten: no one makes it past four, and here we are at seven. The light fades too fast. You come to and there's so much pain contained behind that blood taste. The ward nurse offers you a drink and you wonder why it hurts to swallow and it's two years later that you find the anaesthetist had stuffed a tube down your throat. Good bye, good bye.

McKenzie Wark & Terri-ann White

Game #3

Books and planes go together for me. Or usually they do. This time something caught my attention and wouldn't let it go, pausing concentration like a video still. There was a time when the book was a stationary thing. There was a time when they were chained to monk's desks. To stop them flying away, presumably. Then books became more portable, bound for ship and train. Now they fly with us, too.

Perhaps this is just the book of the west, of which I am thinking. Book of prophets, traversing the desert. Book of abstraction, uprooting gods from their special places, making god and space uniform and empty, leaving us wandering ... the desert now a world. Here and there linger places that have their local gods — or where the powers-that-be mint new ones.

Watching the TV news, en route from Sydney to Melbourne. Watching NATO launch its first air strikes against Serbia, news air time plays host to another kind of strike. Images of what we are told are Tomahawk cruise missiles. They pop from ships like jack-in-the-boxes. Then cut to images of something burning in what we are told is Belgrade, or some other site in Serbia — little brightly coloured maps give a crude approximation of locations. These reports were all vague and sketchy, except concerning the type of weapons used.

I think of my father, building airstrips in New Guinea in the 40s, while my mother worked in an office somewhere, moving the bits of paper around the desk that enabled the stuff of war to be moved all over the Pacific. At least that's what I think they did during the war. I'm sure there's a record of their movements somewhere, too. People, books, missiles, crossing out the blank pages of the world.

Travel isn't valuable until thresholds are crossed or discomforts carried across borders. Until you find the time to consider why you are heading this way. With a good book, a new and engaging one by a beloved writer, at Heathrow, I sit for hours and clock up some of the twenty-seven hours to reach my destination. Watching and listening to the Poms, particularly on the public address, and their visitors. This is now an urgent boarding call. Run, miscreants!

Thinking again about family. The two girls, still teenagers, hopping on a boat to Australia in 1852 and arriving four months later at the height of the West Coast summer. Before tourist slogans, and during a time of punishing and disordered colonial rule. Punishing, anyway, outside of that sphere of influence, if you were a domestic servant, Jewish, young, and escaping something at home in London.

When we arrived we were herded onto buses; it all felt makeshift, this move to our onward connections. Before that, landing onto the gold lights of the imperial city of London as it was coming to life startled me. Then, in an approximation of the journey to a death camp, we are pushed roughly onto these buses and taken around a perimeter. Past smokestacks, vans of all sorts waiting for something or another, waiting to service us. Our coming together is based on mobility; on a choice to move, or necessity; enunciating these details in all of our languages. We are most of us sleepy.

Ours is the century of displacement. Anyone can tell you that. On the radio this morning, in the morass of the mess of current brutalities, we are told of half a million people in Kosovo who are now homeless. Footage last night showed some of them walking away from villages. Where to?

A small blue and red boat breaks the waves, bobbing under a constant sun. Something falls from the boat, a human shape, and floats away. A toy boat, a toy soldier. The girls are indoors, making a home for an eclectically dressed collection of Barbies. The boys are outside, with boats and planes, the backyard and pool their theatre, where soldiers and weapons from several product lines form unlikely battle fronts.

No amount of gentle suggestion or persuasion ever breaks these children out of their gendered worlds. I wonder who, in the long run, comes out better equipped for work and life in the speed factory? Movement is easy now, so much of the jagged line of the world ruled flat. But home, being at home, making oneself at home, making others at home — this is what becomes harder and harder.

They know about home, those Barbies. They encode a weird suburban knowledge of the good life in repose. She may be queerly shaped, oddly coloured, remote from the ambitious flesh of human girls. She may like the trappings of fashion. She may be conflicted about her job and role. But Barbie seems at home in a world without refuge. A world with nowhere to hide hides in her. No Star Wars X-wing fighter can dent her moulded gams.

It was over and gone in a second, a television image, a Barbie in a little girl's hand, as she waits, while her family waits, to cross the border, to escape the war. I think immediately of my niece and her Barbies, and their home under the bed. Words fail me. As mobile as they are, words can only gesture to what is absent in them. They are mobile homes that gesture towards resident referents that they cannot contain.

I scroll through the details of the neighbourhood looking for scandal. Find none: only remnants and legacies. Elizabeth Street. William Street. Birmingham Street. London Street. Rummage through my house looking for something. It might be compassion, it might be a harder edge. Find amusing the little stash of speed and an *e* that I forgot I still had. Am I too old for this caper? That's what I keep asking myself, but what is irresistible is the drama of the rush I recall in a big warehouse, the music filling it, the drive of sex and other pleasure filling it, setting us up. The former furniture factory turned speed terminal. This memory is a conflation of at least four nights, epic night-days. In it the chemicals transform me, as you'd hope they might. Stretch me out, but I'm still fast.

Tonight, in lieu of coffee beans, I begin a sequence: coffee liqueur from Mexico, *koffiewafels* from Holland, iceblocks from the freezer, then down to speed writing and thinking about houses, and privacy. Thinking about my neighbourhood.

A girl named Lisa Brown has been missing for more than this year. She was twenty-one, a mother of two, a street worker in my suburb. Street worker is the euphemism for women who do their business in the front seats of cars parked in laneways around here, or parked right there on the street. Forty bucks a blow job and seventy for the full monty. That's what folks say.

Her boyfriend pimp told no one for nearly a week that

she was missing, and the police took another week to admit she wasn't the nice, funlovin' girl they had set her up to be. And the city erupts into people talking their differences: property values; serial killers; moral imperatives; basic safety matters; heroin trials.

Thinking again about cricket. The English players, young men, hopping on a boat to Australia in 1932 and arriving a few weeks later at the height of the West Coast summer. Before tourist slogans, and during a time of depression and economic uncertainty. A relief, surely, if like fast bowler Larwood you had escaped the coal mines of Nottinghamshire.

The Perth matches were uneventful, but this was the infamous bodyline tour, where English captain Jardine had Larwood bowl what they called 'leg theory'. A fast ball pitched short, bounces high and speeds toward Bradman's body. If he doesn't offer a stroke, it hits him, high on the forward leg. If he strikes, the ball will likely go to the closely placed fielders.

Just not cricket! Ah, but it is. This genteel game that threaded men of empire together revealed its red right hand. The pitch is no safe haven, it bristles with ballistics.

The surprise of it wore off. Ray Robinson could write a decade later, having seen war and empire come and go: 'Nothing the War Office did from 1939 onward puzzled Australians more than the failure to make use of D R Jardine's talent for generalship by setting him up alongside Field Marshall Montgomery (who called his staff his First XI and foretold that he would hit Rommel for six out of Africa).'[26]

The 40s and the 80s, the more I think of it, are the signal decades when the speed factory sped up, when space became consumed and liquefied in the rush to make the world over in its image. In the 40s, it's the metal-bending factories that make a world according to the leg theory of Henry Ford. In the 80s, it's the shrink-wrapped digits of Bill Gates. The 40s and the 80s, amphetamine years.

Tired of the absorption method, of soaking up tonal considerations, pace, paragraphs, pathos, the world of worthy stories, I'm taking off for a sprint. Cranking up the pace, going for a burn. Partner, I'll leave you behind. I am ready again after all of these years. Once upon a time the hurdles star at school, hopeless at everything else, I went at the obstacles without fear, just fast. Up and over. The song 'I can see clearly now' always confused me with its acknowledgment of the obstacles in his way: I wasn't used to such honesty. Come on, girl, with your big claims to speed, get fast! In life I'm fast; when I write it is ponderous, too often ponderous. The speed of the week is liberating me. I want to do my stuff and project into a future perfect. Needing stability in these times. God, that Hüsker Dü version of 'Eight Miles High' has been hitting me since I took up my post in the speed factory. The energy sounds loud; it's a buzz through torso and then legs. I'm dancing, the habitually private dance of the sole occupant/householder. Circling into satisfaction. On the big wooden dance floor at the Passenger Terminal in Fremantle, with everyone else I know from this place, dancing for what might be the first time to Nick Cave and the Bad Seeds, and I'm near my sister and her partner and the floor is bowing so dramatically and we are about two floors up and she says, well, if we go down the children will be all alone. So one of us gets off, goes outside for fresh air to watch the dolphins play at the edge of the sea, and ensure the children their good adult friends. Music makes the world go around.

When did this party start? This dancing world? These creaking timbers, barely holding? Everyone mobilised, meshed for production. I'm reading about the 40s, that time those 60s people never told us about. I'm reading Jean Devanny's *Bird of Paradise*, about the home front.[27] Where even remote and inaccessible forests of North Queensland get drawn into the big bop:

'The primitive and elemental is the original source of victory. In the history of the propeller there comes first of all the searching of the forests for the special timbers which alone can perform and survive critical service.' The forests become a standing reserve, a logistical factor. 'Every board sent down to Aircraft Production carries on it the number of the log from which it was cut and that log number is an index of its place of origin, its location there, its kind of soil, its stance, whether straight or leaning, its position, sheltered or exposed. In short, its log number is a dialectical record of the tree.'

This resource, borne away from the forest, is of unknown value — until it reaches the Aircraft Production, where 'each board is subjected to the most rigid mechanical laboratory tests.' Here the raw material has added to it information about its properties. 'Of the timbers so laboriously won from nature's treasure house, the proportion finally used in the propeller may be less than one per cent of the original log volume.' The war machine includes a complex process of categorising timber and assigning it to a use, depending on its properties.

'Organisation holds the trump card.' In principle, nothing should be wasted, although the honest writer in Jean Devanny cannot quite submit to the organisation of the text around the war aims. In this wayward writing, little facts — chaos and fuck-ups — foul the factory.

Forgive me as I pre-empt even my own steps. Dancing ahead of time. I write because I have to, getting a tired body out of bed to sit and compose and dream of dance, awake, and then lose the draft and then find it intact, and then follow multiple threads of music across my life and over the World Wide Web. And then find your night's work, read it and see the congruence, the red right hand, the move out of an utterly un-danceable Cave period right into do you love me? So I send. Is it just the two years between our birthdays that throws up such chance? Every time I obsessively check my words, obediently, disciplined, I get the count at a hundred and six. Is this the first pause, the breath-point? Today is a day not to think about vacuum cleaner factories with a workforce of five thousand pummelled into the ground by, presumably, Nighthawk stealth fighters. I dunno. It's a holiday, not even a newspaper to refer to. Pristina. Such a pretty name. Do they know it's Easter?

Bill T Jones motion-captures his dancing, choreographed body, and then other artists do things with it: drawings, computer compositions.[28] Separated from musculature and the mass of what is usually there, it becomes ghost-trading; movement and the body different elements. These ghosts multiply and dance together, dance Jones's choreography. He has removed the flesh and blood, banished that; showing only lines and paths that are left, a decommissioned living: traces, crystalline threads on the edges of former body occupation. I'm distracting myself with questions about traces, the ghostliness left behind for us to meddle with. Numbers on logs, the origins clearly stated and detectable; the history of horrors, painstakingly documented. In this wayward world, little facts — chaos and fuck-ups — foul our factory.

Motion capture — isn't that what this half century is all about? Motion capture — such a useful word bequeathed by the digital techheads. Motion capture — the tape rolls snap-freezes Charlie Parker's alto break. Separated from musculature and the mass of what is usually there, it becomes ghost-trading; movement and the body different elements.

This feels more like jazz than dancing. Riffing on great old mid-century tunes. The ones that code for the new world, then yet to come. Kenneth Slessor, Australia's Official War Correspondent, records the work and days of No. 10 Squadron of the RAAF. The reports are motion capture: 'With their detailed masses of figures and code letters they look more like mathematical propositions ... senior airmen of the squadron have to combine the violence and adventure of actual operations with the executive office work of preparing charts, logs, statistics and other reports.'[29]

The *Operations Record Book* is an alien literature. 'Here in clipped, official sentences, as curtly scientific as a cardiograph, the living history of the squadron is laid bare. Masses of mathematical detail tell the story of all aircraft flown, of every bomb dropped or lost ...'

A writing of a world yet to come, which we now know too well. 'At first, reading these bald statements of height, speed and temperature, of miles covered and work done, one almost loses a sense of that reality which they so dispassionately record. But behind each line, if you pause, you can hear the wind screaming and see the skyline rolling itself up like a map and the grey waters flowing continually underneath. Infinities of sea and air are compressed into the curt entry: "Patrol safely carried out".' Not many of Slessor's despatches made it into print back in Australia. Ahead of their time. Premature motion capture.

There is a recording made in 1957 of Thelonious Sphere

Monk playing with John Coltrane at the Five Spot in New York. Late summer, the recording device a portable tape with a single microphone belonging to Naima, John's wife at the time. The balance and sound quality is certainly an impediment, but what cannot be doubted, not for a minute, is that those guys were flying. Raw, elemental sound laid over with the extraordinary lexicon of abstraction that Monk carried in his head all his life. The piano sounds like he is playing his teeth. Coltrane blows like the wigged-out master he was, these long phrases, breath-in-the-body virtuosic signature. Ira Gitler calls it 'sheets of sound — the technique of playing double, triple and quadruple time, using irregular fast clumps of notes in order to explore several possibilities over each chord.'[30] I can see Monk sitting there, weighing it all up; in control, but you might not be able to tell that until he began to play. Coltrane recovering again from smack and on the edge of exhaustion, but this was his turning-point year, the year his habit broke. Enjoying a gig with Monk for some of its fringe benefits, the benefactor Baroness for one with her 'scotch that flowed in a stream.'

What of the note that a part of 'Epistrophy' is missing because it was recorded over at a later date? I remember recording myself singing 'Harper Valley PTA' on a little portable machine. We finish with 'Crepuscule with Nellie', delicately; this time the producer informs that this was what opened the set. They have to let us wind down at the end of the CD: it's that fast and furious. By the way, the executive producer is T S Monk, the son and a minor funkster from an earlier time.

Playing more Monk and Coltrane while I pack my books in boxes. It's a rare studio recording, from the same period.[31] Monk approaches 'Nutty' as deconstruction, picking apart his own melody, spinning new stings of notes out of folds in the tune, the melodic order undone and undone again. A lot of what passes for deconstruction in critical writing strikes me, by comparison, as sounding more like those endless guitar solos in 70s 'progressive rock' — so much technique wasted with so little to show for it.

Monk was present at the creation, playing with Bird and Diz at Mintons in the 40s, present for that moment when the melodic fabric unravelled in Bird's hands, exposing the harmonic threads from which it was made, the fibre of American music, from which new claddings could be made.

On those 40s recordings, its all pure speed, intense elaborations on merry melodies, so many ideas crammed onto a 78 rpm disc. By the 50s, the long playing 33 rpm disc opened a space for a new art form — the jazz recording, on which Coltrane could blow for twenty minutes at a stretch.

Packing books, the dust making me sneeze. Silverfish resent this redevelopment of their neighbourhood. All these paper books and vinyl records, pounds of dead men's flesh. I'm working up a sweat lugging this patrimony. Oh, there is the dead breath of women, too, from Virginia Woolf to Ella Fitzgerald, but I think of all this mass, this weight of information as the rock they tried to roll from their path.

Perhaps we're of an age to be on the cusp. Children of the analogue age, soaking since birth in television and radio and big black records. Immersed from childhood in all that the manufacturing revolution of the 40s delivered to the suburban home.

Skipping ahead again and it's worth it, for me anyway. Pre-emptive strikes, following my fancies. I got caught up with Monk in the afternoon, write before my turn, save it for later, go to a party next door: all gay men, about fifty of them, and three other women, but I'm used to this. I'm reliably told the others are fag hags or straight, and I have no reason to doubt. But tiring of the scene of cigarettes and chunky men wanting to be svelte, and wanting my own music back — more, more — I slip out quietly, end up eating Japanese, and getting the coffee beans I have needed for days now. Then home. And there was Ken: This feels more like jazz than dancing.

I open a new document: Good Friday.

With their detailed masses of figures and code letters they look more like mathematical propositions. So he just stands up and moves away from the piano. And begins to dance. Spinning around, a spastic dance as they would have once said. Shuffling, arms akimbo, looking like a man who has never danced before. Someone else is soloing so it's okay, not a dereliction of duty. Can you hear the silence in his composition and in his playing? You turn some of those corners, or angles, in his work and sometimes there is a sacred space of silence, a respite. Singing to you, if only you know what you are looking for. Like brilliant corners. Art Blakey with his sexy percussive work, knowing properly Monk's shapes, filling up some of those spaces with delicate colours. I wanna hold your hand.

But it is the big man in his funny hat dancing as if he might fall over at the front of the stage that I want to end with. Be careful opening documents — the Melissa virus is out to get you! Newspapers with screamer headlines warn that the BAD GIRL is on the loose. Love the way the print media misses no opportunity to demonise its electronic rival, the internet. The internet isn't the information superhighway in newspaper diction, but a back alley infested with virus-laden crackhead whores called Melissa.

This fusing of information and virus in the demonology of the times — I just watched another *X Files* video, which has this down cold. Phillip Adams may rail against this show, but really, its the only one that tells the truth. An unelected, unrepresentative, unaccountable, self-appointed elite, who use information and bio-technology to advance their power, but who are really just the agency driving the world towards a posthuman future, where we are transformed even faster than before, so fast that we no longer recognise ourselves in the mirror, or even in the mirror of art. The truth really is out there. The military entertainment complex even makes a show about it.

And of course, in the epic saga of the *X Files*, it all begins in the 40s — the coming together of centralised state, corporate and military power. Built to fight off fascism, but which became what it beheld. Only more subtle, diffuse, centreless and leaderless. Not a conspiracy, just a new way of life. One dedicated to making the world over, one product at a time. Everything a potential input; no limit to the potential outputs.

And this way of life is not a bad life. I eat Japanese take out to Thelonious on cd, pure popless sound. And in Monk you can hear it — this world in which there are so many possibilities, where even a simple tune hides sublime concertinas folded within.

Melissa isn't the only girl on the block, isn't the only virus running rampant. Don't forget the April Fool's shows. Out to humiliate their work colleagues, middle managers become lame in the face of one joke they might do well. Ritual humiliations are really just good fun, bloody good fun on that one day of the year. I wish that I could push a button and talk in the past and not the present tense, and watch this hurting feeling disappear like it was common sense.[32]

The hardest thing for me is to hold it all together, bunched up to my breast, the precious harvest of these yearnings and satisfactions together, little losses and big ones, hard to not explode with joy. Hard-earned joy, I hope; all about observations and observances, influences and pleasures, confluences and the critical mass that has allowed me to move through the multiple doors I have of education, mobility, confidence, choice. To this. To be able to say, I am a writer and what I do is write. My Jewish forebears used incantations to remember the dead. Nowadays we swallow names. Stay silent. Implode with our knowledge of specific pain and what is no longer there. The absence of nourishment.

But not me: I'm gathering up some of my pleasures to keep going with. Thelonious Monk, Eric Dolphy, but whatever you do DON'T get me started. Everything a potential input, and as we know, intimately, there is no limit to the potential outputs.

I was thinking that I don't know anyone who was actively adult in the 40s, and then I remembered how surprised I was last year and this year to find how many people I know or love were born in 1948 and 1949. But even my parents weren't adults until the 50s. And all the more reason to try and evoke the 40s, while people who remember that time are still with us. They won't be with us for long. And we won't be around for long, either. Others will come along and question what we chose to pass on to them, in turn, too.

There's something strange about Easter in Australia. The eggs and bunnies, images of new life, celebrated in autumn, time of decline. Is there any choice but to take it ironically? Visiting friends and chewing on the hot cross buns, I couldn't help but reflect on things, anyway, on beginnings and ending, making and unmaking.

A pessimist by nature, I found a cheery mask for social occasions. But the mask became part of my face. And so, mask and all, I try to keep dancing. Joy would be the word for it, had it not fallen into decline in the English language. The joy of going down to the river, the river of Heraclitus, the river of Al Green. All-moving river, immersing and all moving. There's nothing constant in this life, only things that move very, very slow. Wash me in the water ...

Packing my library in crates, I pack my Walter Benjamin, and resist a temptation to flop on the lounge and read Benjamin's essay on packing his library. I think instead of those little houses in Amsterdam. They line the canals of the old city. Each has an arm projecting from the eaves with a pulley, on which to haul furniture—the stairs are too narrow to move even a chair. I can only marvel at the genius of a people who can make buildings that honestly announce the temporary nature of all that passes through them. Buildings which, appropriately enough, have now survived centuries.

A mask of joy, a time to ask questions. This tripping across words, this selecting, carefully, and throwing back at each other; the game across a telephone line with words, is something I haven't done for a while. The only way I can recall doing it anyway is as part of conflict with lovers and best friends, that throwing action, a backhander, involving quotation, selective, but often in whole chunks of text memorised, bloodily.

But we don't know each other. So how does it feel for you? What is this vector product that you are currently living in like? For me it is surprisingly scintillating: I, looking forward to your words, am ranging as wide as ever in anticipation. Jumping ahead of myself. Pleased to have been home more than I usually am.

Two films, two parties. Cherry ice-cream, my current favourite, with both of the films. I bought some tonight for home, but it is much more sophisticated than the cinema version, which is entirely a nostalgic trip. This is my yield for the weekend. And twenty hours of government work, cleaning up a bad general history of the women of this state. It'll get me a trip around the world, and such invitations always makes me feel like an infiltrator. Working editorially just with tone, to salvage their propaganda.

Of course you want to know the two films (don't you?). The *Exterminating Angel* and *Lolita*. Buñuel hypnotised me this time, I couldn't keep my eyes open; it was a fight and I wasn't even tired. *Lolita* better than I expected: in a cinema of people thrilled to be transgressing, it took me back to sneaking a look at Portnoy's juicy confessions at twelve under my mother's bed.

Must your books go in crates?

(Thank you for Al Green.)

'Having nothing to write about (nothing particular to write about) suggests a question: what this morning do you particularly not want to say?'[33]

Harry Mathews, from *20 Lines A Day*. The title comes from Stendhal: 'twenty lines a day, genius or not.' That's how Stendhal got his art history stuff written. Mathews uses the technique to write, not about something else, but about the day itself, and the lines, and the 'or not'.

'Is writing less a part of life than talking on the phone? Than riding in taxicabs? Than taking naps?' I'm quoting Harry to draw another voice into the conversation. 'Writing is the translation of one body into another.' Only most usually, for me, this writing by email — it's a translation of a translation. It's the letters of lovers, spiralling around each other, quoting each other, tugging on the body via the screen, via flows of photons, electrons.

It never works.

Neither does writing to strangers who might, in the abstract, share an interest. Unless it happens to be the writing itself. Maybe that's what *Speed Factory* was always all about: making a way of making that would have the medium itself as its inexhaustible source.

'What matters is to address, unhurriedly and without

procrastination, the page that, because it is the first of many to be faced during the day, is the most discouraging and the most liberating. After all, it is nothing but the happiness of writing that awaits me.'

Why should that source of joy not be shared? Words poured into the modem that seek another object of desire, emotional or sexual, they miss their mark. Not the joy of writing itself. No book you can buy will set you free, redeem your hopes, refloat your love boat. Reading incites no satisfaction other than writing.

No book you can buy will set you free, redeem your hopes, refloat your love boat. Refloat your love boat — did I type that! Reading incites no satisfaction other than writing. It starts with a sighting of thick ankles, a trademark of the women down the generations of family, through a sea of legs and feet. A recognition. Doesn't matter where this happens, far from home; the distance is probably what makes it work, what makes it potent.

I am in a Russian bar in New York City, the Russian Samovar, listening to a poetry recital. Because I arrived late I am trapped on the staircase up to the performance space. But I can see the poet's face and hear clearly his words, and am faced with a room filled with legs under tables. Here is a pair of legs enclosed in school-supply grey stockings with ankles that are solid, as impressive as a horse's fetlocks. A private peepshow, seen only by me. They take me back to home, to Perth and the site of family. When I was a girl I was appalled at the idea that I would follow into this monstrosity at their age: that my legs would grow into horse's legs.

Thankfully they haven't, but for a while it was a spooky idea.

Wasn't Harry's Bar in Venice named after Harry Mathews? Or am I mixing my muscular-man-writing figures? I went in to pay homage to something: my literary heritage, perhaps, but it was too fucking smoky for my good. Anyway, I already do that regime of words every day and now I'm doing it with a stranger.

Here is what I am doing: making a way of making that would have the medium itself as its inexhaustible source. Now: Elizabeth Bishop! She refloats my love boat.

By chance, it's a book I've not packed away: Victor Shklovsky's account of Mayakovsky's life, loves, work and suicide: 'He died, having surrounded his death like a disaster area with warning lights; he died, having explained how the love boat crashes, how man perishes, not of unrequited love, but because he has ceased loving.'[34]

I was attached to those revolutionary Russians of the 20s once, but I gave them up, gave their books away. I kept Victor because he displayed more sense, in difficult times, than the others.

A sinister face watched me from the walls, walking

around in New York. I was there at the time of the big Rodchenko show at MOMA. The poster for it was his portrait of Osip Brik, whose wife Lili Mayakovsky loved, and ceased to love. Brik gave up art and literature and joined the CHEKA, forerunner of the KGB. This didn't surprise me. There was something rotten at the core of those modern-isms for which Brik was just a bit too enthusiastic.

It's when things crash that they reveal the accident waiting in them all along. Accidents of love, war, of genetic inheritance. These club feet of mine, attached to skinny ankles, they are my accidental inheritance. This war in Europe — the Serbian Socialist Party holding out against NATO's imperium.

People can choose to (pro)create their descendants, but have no choice about having ancestors. With writers, it is the other way around.

Which leaves the problem, as a writer, of a double belonging, of belonging by blood and belonging by words. I'm just not convinced these should have much to do with each other. I don't want to make words that are trapped by accidents of identity, but rather which escape it, which seep and lodge elsewhere in the world.

I want to make words that are not trapped by accidents of identity, but rather which escape it, which seep and lodge elsewhere in the world, by telling the grand secrets, by animating those secrets. This isn't nostalgic yearning but I hope a harder kind of yearning that opens up some of the spaces of family, of precious lives that came before me. When nothing has been passed down, not even the ankles, I am obliging myself to dredge things up.

Elizabeth Bishop starts the poem with:

The art of losing isn't hard to master; so many things seem filled with the intent to be lost that their losing is no disaster.[35]

And my Word program wants to clean up her punctuation. It's late, and I'm yearning: this time something quite out of my grasp. Something coiling out of my chest. I wish that it were something easy like being lonely: it is much deeper than that. The reminders of dissolutions and true terror, of everything changing; they keep coming in, on the hour, through the wireless.

She feels mortality on her skin: she wears it; it is a cloak, close fitting. Not oppressive, though, just resonant and reverent. People came before her. Some, her peers, also suffered early deaths and some are suffering still. The cloak protects and reminds her of real pleasure, of acquaintance, of intimacies that follow friendship and love.

So which way to the making of the family picture? Impossible to choose, so I set off in one direction and then another. I begin to tell a granddaughter's story. But there is too much already to do in a life without digging up the past. Too much suffering without wilfully digging it up, without forcing people to relive that pain. The art of losing isn't hard to master.

Here is what I want: a desire to make a way of making that would have the medium itself inexhaustibly. Like the erotic repertoire of lovers who go for years and years. Finding rhythms that sustain each other: fast slow fast. The variety is inexhaustible. Getting used to quirks, tics, petty annoyances; staying in that grand drama: love, erotic attachment. What I am fantasising about isn't ever habitual, premeditated.

Writing my primary erotic expression now, entering into new spaces and explorations. The making, over and again; the erotics of learning and testing out this, and then that. It is spreading all over this joy, my face now pink, I am primed, opened up. What began it all was the bright bone of a dream I could hardly hold onto.[36]

The utility of language. The bare bones of that dream. The return back to a former place, an earlier self, a happier time, or even more confusion. None of that ever matters. Telling it first in a plain and everyday form and then transforming. Some real things have happened lately.[37] The sentence, in its closure and its 'neatness', seems to me, then, the fundamental determination of writing.[38]

Driving around the river, the winding road between escarpment and water. The light is leaving the sky, the water glistening in the way you imagine it does in a dream. The sky is leached of all late-day colour and now it is the palest shade of, what? How could you describe that? As if in a dream, it's so soft you could wrap yourself in it because you have never seen anything so extraordinary. A shade of salmon, but not pink. I dare you to describe it.

— Even losing you (the joking voice, a gesture I love) I shan't have lied.[39]

John Kinsella & Terri-ann White

Game #4

They'd dumped the case on me. I was going to throw it right back in their faces when a name caught my attention. It took me back, and I didn't like it. The evening was still and cold. She'd called it crisp. I'd lit the fire and then those lines from Gertrude Stein's *Stanzas in Meditation* cracked out of the flames: 'It is very often that they like to care/That they have it there that the window is open/If the fire which is lit and burning well/Is not open to the air.'[40] It's not true, she said and wandered over to check the window. She hesitated, the curtains draped around her, the half-light tugging at her. What's wrong? I asked, picking up on her discomfort. It's out there, on the hilltop, watching us. Again. It had been months. Seasons back since we'd last seen it. On an evening just like this when those lines of Stein's leapt out of the fire. I kept reading through the file. I couldn't turn it down, and they knew it.

The storm blowing all around me, the tempest of uncertainty. Nothing compares to you. In that cylinder of curtain, of drape; your body so expertly cloaked, you look out the window and notice how the main drama of the night is playing out in your body. That strength cannot be matched by anything else: not wind, not pounding rain. The word that looms, one you have not thought of for a lifetime, but still it seems to fit. *Corpuscle.*

A relation to a body, to a fire and a set of words about a fire; the moon is out, out there, and here you are, being loved. Internal combustion always sounds inadequate to that fire, that setting-on-fire of a couple of bodies matched with a purpose. It's a fire, a frisson, a dream of desire. And then it happens. Crisp and, finally, satisfying. So thanks for the memory. The sheer sweep of the words as they whip around me. 'I am I and my name is Marguerite Ida and Helena Annabel, and then oh then I could yes I could I could begin to cry but why why could I begin to cry ... (In the distance there is daylight and near to there is none.)[41] They asked about clues and I said you're missing the point. This isn't a case about clues. But what about these lines: 'Be made to ask my name. If I think well of him be made to ask my name'? It's stanza LXIX, I said. It's not a clue, I added for good measure. You seem drained of emotion, a mere shell. That's just my manner. I could sense they were trying to drag something out of me, to build a profile not of the victim but me. I guess I had it coming. Never turning up at office parties, refusing to join the circulating joke. That kind of thing. And yet, that fire and window and that point at the top of the hill, as the light was fading, comes back again and again. I see myself at that point. Distance clarifies. Duration is essentially memory, consciousness and freedom.[42] The genetically modified crops move towards … ripeness? A bit of each of us in them. The chain, the cycle. I don't buy any of it. When I say, Give me a Martini! I mean give me a damned Martini. Nothing more, nothing less. Shaken not stirred shaken not stirred shaken not stirred comes the mantra. The steroids kick in and the hurdles seem less of a problem. Just lines in the barcode. It burns within us, she said. Within you, I said. I postured for the sake of memory, for the old ways. 'I'll tell me ma when I go home/ the boys won't leave the girls alone/ they pulled my hair and they stole my comb/ well that's all right till I go home.' That's the joke, and I don't get it.

I get it all. I insist on the getting. Is that duration or endurance. Pulling myself through clues, through fields filled with fluff. Some sticks, some wind up my nose. I am insistent and in the end I always get my way, find the path and avoid resistance. Stanzas are good for some purposes, and clues guide us well in our sleep, but I won't be a victim again. It's sad enough to watch the half living; hell, we don't have time. We need this push and sometimes the push is entwined with the Campari, sometimes it is autonomous. Once upon a time I read an alarming tale of betrayal and after that time I memorised it, rehearsed it, and now I know it backwards. The denouement comes fast and is relatively painless at version #376. Sometimes I wonder about repetition, about the madness of posting numbers on the board and then trying to remember necessary sequencing. As long as it doesn't keep you awake all day I'd say, my old boy, you should do it. To the maximum effect will do, and jolly good company.

But then doubt creeps in again. I return to Deleuze on Bergsonism. Not that it's a crutch, but an inevitability. I sense myself dividing into indefinable parts. I am bright in the loungeroom, dull in the bar. I read, or say, for example: '... at each instant pure duration divides in two directions, one of which is the past ...' and I'm there, at the fireside, again. They came the next day and burnt the house to the ground. I said, this is an extension of our activities. Our flesh seared together. I carry her with me and now I'm supposed to be on her trail. Or on the retrail of a memory. I'm writing my own obituary, and there is some pleasure in this: '... the other the present; or else the élan vital at every instant separates into two movements, one of relaxation (détente) that descends into matter, the other of tension that ascends into duration.' And it was here that I reversed gender, upset the plot. They wanted to assign an extra. I told them. No, I'm telling them, the stage isn't big enough for both of us. Two seniors melding in and on the one case, persisting in their prejudices, hungry to feed their hunches. We are both the same height, same weight. Sexual proclivity uncertain.

In dreams the sadnesses arrive, multiple, weighty. None of them about specifics; they don't need to be. The storm reaches some point of utter madness outside my head and so I sleep poorly all this night. I am sure the house will be blown away, that all my confidences in a secure future will be damaged. Miles upon miles of tarpaulins covering people's precious living spaces, their collections of comfort. The albums of photographs that will now and forever curl at the edges, look less because of the tint of dampness. I am being blown this way and that. Decide against an obituary for anyone at all, but especially not for me. The smooth surfaces of a box seem appealing; I need rest, need to remake this trajectory of flesh, of complementarity, of equivalent measurement. Where to from here? The bush track seems an option at last, for the first time. Getting lost in deserts is no great drama, more a communicating impulse, a madness worth owning. This desert is big enough for the both of us, but let's walk in opposite directions. Should I begin to tell of my sexual proclivities, begin to reveal myself and my needs? That is a decision still to be made. I remake myself.

She's come in now, fully. Speaking with my voice, I with hers. They'll have me up in front of internal affairs over this. Complicit before I begin. It's the genre that has me say, I'm being consumed. I'm aware. The investigation spawns metatext. The Holocene. All of it leading to this. Year after year. The calendar kicks in and we watch the months flutter to the ground like dry leaves. It's a cheap picture. The nitrate film is decaying, sticking to itself. The rot of a Shepherd's calendar. Let's just suppose the collusion of hill and domestic bliss was a dream. Let's suppose the intrusion was something hoped for, desired. The fire's warmth a pheromonal trigger. Mary Daly has been locked out of her room. A right-wing thinktank is backing the moves of her enemies. She takes a leave of absence. The Jesuits are keeping quiet and the Vatican is unmoving.

Unflinching. I know someone down in Files who can check on this. Not everything has found its way into computers yet. The city is short on cash and this is a job that'll take years. I'll have long gone by the time they get to D for Daly. They're still thinking about A. Built-up areas no more than rubble. The tarpaulins don't keep us out. The eye of the camera takes a sneak preview. I go through the photographic evidence. There, there's something we've missed. A slight blurring to the left of the body. This is the desert in the discourse. The blank. The shifting emptiness.

This is where we meet, despite walking in opposite directions. It is the point of rapture and of tragedy. Chandler writes, in this dusty place: 'His cigarette was jiggling like a doll on a coiled spring.' The duration of the scene is measurable in terms of heat. Celsius, Fahrenheit, Kelvin, joule, calorie. Absolute zero. By degrees. That's just before dawn and the storylines freeze over and fuse. We become articulations of derivative tales. The subplots come into their own. I keep a straight face, though inside my nerves are getting the better of me. This isn't about the nature of a relationship with the case, with the crime. There's a bunch of us having tea in the office and we look out of the window onto a hill. A light glints in a window opposite. The hard baked among us take two lumps of sugar. It provides energy. We move faster away from each other in this widening investigation. Tomorrow I'll take the case to the prosecutor. The air will be thick with smog and electricity. There's powder in the air. Late summer storms. The desert is turning to plaster, sticking hard to the skin. You can taste it. You can taste the oxidation of sulphur. Which takes me back even further, right back to the day before we met: the gardens were lush, but dust had found its way into the city.

I left the body out in the cold one more time. There is something to be said for practice, for staying in the world of sex and its concomitant pleasures, its way of teaching you how to be with people, with letting down barriers between talk and touch. Once, you know, she went out of her mind worrying about whether it would ever be possible to be like that again: malleable, open, casual about her body and about how pleasure might be activated and then lived with. The man in the brown suit sitting at that table on the edge of the room, a room of cooked food and beverages, of cordiality and sociable choice — he knows all about this. I knew him once and in a brief encounter I learnt a great deal about loss and how to live with it. A range of barriers were dissolved in a brief encounter; the calendar was made inexplicable and the shape of a life was given a new constitutive power. This was all liberating, no doubt about that. Leaving all of us frail but smarter by the end of it. The leave of absence lasts for about a year and contains many conditions. Don't forget any of them because if you do you forfeit all that came before. Once a word was uttered in the dining room of food and conviviality and that one word took her on a path that lasted for years, many years. The word? Holocene. She so far has not come out alive, but she will.

And when the push comes to shoving and all of the players are in the cold and none of them are what you'd call satisfied, even properly alive, it is then that it seems the time might have been reached when it has to be abandoned, all of it, and left for dead. Not sustainable. Once upon a time there was a figure in the street and that was a time of fear. It was unclear what the motives of this figure might be. It did not even matter, really; what was invoked was terror and a cowering away from life. I know this might sound like melodrama, but really it was a political matter of the most profound urgency and import. Unbelievable images came to her at night and the building was a concrete heap without windows. It looked like a torture centre and it was hard to dismiss. Why else would they build it with such strong messages, such totalitarianism? If I tell you this is Australia in the late 90s, right at the end of all of this centurying, would you believe me? Could you? Well, it depends upon what you do with your paranoia. Hers was fully fledged: total.

Bernard Cohen & Terri-ann White

Game #5

Uncle, break up the party. Once upon a time I would have let you get away with it, but now it is just too late for any of this. Gnashing of teeth will get you nowhere and will cost you later. Would you like me to describe myself now that you have lost your sight? It will be my pleasure, I love this sort of thing.

So, here I go: wallflower, pretty tall, about five six. When I grow up I'll be a whopper. Freckles everywhere, running all over my face and shoulders. There are teeth in my mouth and they seem still to be growing, down, pearly white. My skin is starting to wear out, paper-thin, easily wounded. Against all the odds I keep on.

Will you tell me about yourself? I'm a good sort in the morning, a witch by the middle of the day, a hard-working beast all night. Started out a foundling. They lost the way and I had to imagine my path. And I did. Turning the form around on its head, turning on the edge of a knife. Everything is related, so why not acknowledge it right at the start. The great excitement happened yesterday when the postcard finally arrived. That photograph of the horse: I knew him in a prior life. Loved him, once, for his qualities.

Every idea a new idea, but now you've got to get thinking and make your own abstractions. The woman talks on and on, deliberately, but she is not deliberate in her gender blindness. She forgot that there was a single other woman in the world. She surely was enough. Deliberate about space, but not about travel. A traveller across inspiration and discipline; her own disciple. Writing as a meditation on life. 'Tomorrow: Dentistry; cake-eating.'

'Hoo boy, I had a feeling you were going to be difficult,' he said, talking all the more slowly. He — twenty-seven, tall, someone who always looked as though he had recently lost weight (people commented), not exactly beautiful, but with a particular gap-toothed appeal he liked to think of as Chaucerian, aquiline nose, wistfully uneven eyebrows, a fleck of green in his blue eyes (this was something his male and female patients always noticed, but they couldn't see the gap in the teeth, the fine nose), a dentist who liked to leave work at work, or so he said, and unlike his medical colleagues he was unlikely to be bailed up with symptoms at a party (more possible at the gym, but no one knew him) — couldn't stand the talkers, delighted in making them help him out by holding the instruments hard against the tongue, made a point of saying this won't take long, perhaps an unpleasant man, probably unpleasant (ask his ex-wife, whose teeth are now green, such was the extent of her anger with Everything He Stood For), certainly unpleasant you think, as you hold the icecream stick against your tongue, which in this situation does feel uncontrollable, is wriggling from side to side despite your conscious effort, and you imagine him blinded, the mask pulled up and over his eyes, your mouth clogged with instruments; and the pair of you are the two wise monkeys, no, the two idiot pigs — you for choosing this dentist (too young, too arrogant), him, well, it's obvious why he's in the category, and the light's shining in your eyes, and he's talking about anaesthetic top-ups, and you're thinking about a friend of the family who wanted to write, who wrote you a picture postcard from Cairo, the home of dentistry.

People are trying to remember when they first read Shakespeare, what it was like at school. Some of them secretly pissed off, right off, that their pet hate is now the big fad. That those wankers with good memories, with all those rote skills, can now look all smoochy in public as they recite that sonnet, number 106 as I recall, that they had learned way back when during the voice training, for a while the preferred career path. You recall the little worm, even then, reciting it at a party to his girlfriend and everyone showing their appreciation and respect, a private moment for fifty bedraggled and perplexed arts students, filmmakers, hippies. No wonder she went over to the other side, found a girlfriend of her own. Of course, he followed; too lonely there by himself, obliged to declare at some stage — well, yes, I think I'm that way too. What do you think? Mister predictable. All I wanted was to listen to that pumping song again, who was it? I think it was Blondie but I could be wrong.

Wasted on the dentistry gas in the back yard, the cylinder supplied by the medical students, I did a dance behind the outhouse. All by myself. My preferred arrangement. Years later at parties, I'm the youngest and unable to hide or dance alone. Back to this drip reciting sonnets. Reminiscence is the name of the game tonight. The woman from Piedmont, beautiful still, tells me about coming to Perth at sixteen and falling in love with a man on the spot. She thought she was coming down with a fever but it was love. Couldn't even walk: the love cut off her legs at the knees. This was in 1951. She still loves her man.

He too, the dentist, is recollecting nitrous. He's twenty again, squatting in a warehouse in Newtown which will soon be serviced apartments. He's thinking about dentistry: should he enrol — would it be just *too* responsible? He sucks on the soda siphon and laughs. 'Dentistry,' he says to Carol, as she inhales.

'Fucking hell,' she splutters. 'You're going to fucking kill me.'

He loved all the hippies, but once he started the course, they abandoned him, despite him filling his parties with nitrous cylinders and the best northern English dance music. ('Hate that London shit.') He was wrong about his friends, about his life, about his good-looker appeal. Nothing overcame dentistry.

'Suction, please,' he says to his assistant, then: 'I'm going to ask you to be really still for a few more moments. I'll just be few more minutes.'

She makes an assenting noise. You can keep them quiet, but you can't tell what they're thinking; the way they look up at you, expressionless, as you lever out a molar, or what's left of it. This one — the woman, not the tooth — seems to be a thinker, always careful with opinions during the small talk.

Looks vaguely familiar, but who can tell?

'This is a little deeper than I'd initially thought,' he says, 'so I'm going to strengthen the anaesthesia. I'd like you to close your eyes and try to relax.'

She's feeling okay, but then he starts: 'How many thousand of my poorest subjects Are at this hour asleep! O sleep! O gentle sleep! Nature's soft nurse, how have I frighted thee, That thou no more wilt weigh my eyelids down And steep my senses in forgetfulness?'

'Jesus Christ,' she tries to say, forgetting, as the blues and pinks, fathoms down into the dental lamp, begin to whirl.

I'll take you anywhere you want to go. On a nostalgia trip

this week, a return to sites of pleasure. Hell, that's all I do, hang around and find pleasure. Embedded. Going back to music that made me what I am; some of the influential streams that have stayed with me even when I haven't kept listening. Looking through my dinosaur collection of long-playing vinyl, I realise that nearly any one of them can be recalled, played out in my head, with more clarity than back then. Says something about this brilliant adventure of a life. Half of the Go-Betweens in a smoky crowded bar, just the boys. With two guitars and two voices they cook up a storm of remembering, and some longing. And so now I'm back to those old songs of yearning, and identifying with their small-city experience of writing a picture of home.

Behind me the two men have a conversation about boats, buying and selling, racing and the club, and they are so close their breath drops down onto my head. It isn't offensive, but it is surprisingly intimate. Perth is a city that sanctions sailing, its incongruity: this music, that sporting class-ridden pursuit, is maybe only in my head. This was the home of the America's Cup.

At the Billy Bragg concert another night this week the ghosts of my past came crashing in: one, a man I once tried to fuck in a car, in the front seat, parked outside his parents' house in the cold light of dawn. You can tell he now wishes he'd tried harder back then.

Sometimes dentistry makes him want to cry; his eyes fill. He thinks of his former friends whirling, spinning, remembering, and is overcome with remorse because he need not remember, he need only look up to see what others must recall in their minds. He could cry in his surgery as the CD slides in and plays the tunes he listened to, and he has never listened to anything else. His life is a life of dental modalities. He has befriended other dentists. He is the most morose of all his acquaintances and bloody well knows it. Patients file past, and he is as if on autopilot, as if travelling through the air at speed, the days a blur, every molar like every other, impaction after impaction, all the tiny haemorrhages of unhealthy gums, and always he winds up thinking of regrets, this woman in the chair who does not recognise him, that the skills to which he has devoted his life — spent his life practising, rather, he corrects himself bitterly — that these are the skills his patients take to be mechanical, skills any dentist should possess, and for once he decides to be the one to move, and he tells his patient she is to be his last patient, and that he will give it all up although he has nothing to go to, no way to take his life 'forward', no momentum but that provided by his knowledge of the history of dental anaesthesia (nitrous: Humphrey Davey, 1799; common in clinical practice by the late 1840s ...) and he offers, 'rinse?' for the last time, and she spits out, wisp of saliva which will not drop from her lip enclosing traces of blood, and she says, 'Thank you, dentist' with respect for what he had been. He is crying.

And I am in denial. The teeth are on the verge of falling out. That is how it feels, anyway. I cannot deal with the emotional range that seems to be required to make an appointment, so nightly I dream of the teeth in a life of their own. By the way, I also dream of football. Footballers and their bodies, whacking each other by accident, taking an elbow-full of pearly white teeth to the turf. The blood follows, the crowd roars. At home, on the television, his mother recalls what had been sacrificed to get those lovely milky teeth straightened. The years of bus trips to the orthodontist in Saint George's Terrace. The expense, the resentments of the other children to the special attention to Tommy's mouth, the little rubber bands he was supposed to clasp to the contraption of his mouth and that ended up all over the house.

Last night I went to a nightclub in a five-star hotel, modelled on a shiny silver disco from another age. It included in the back of the back bar a big silver bed with console lights and the rest of the gear. I was tempted: a love-in might have been fun, but there was no one to fuck anyway. Three big fish tanks, well appointed; no easy escapes. Proponents of noise, Merzbow, from Japan. It was loud but not that loud. Everybody fixated by claims of 'the loudest' wore the earplugs offered at the door. The earplugs our focus. It was ghastly, this desire to talk about what wasn't important. So loud that people gestured, to their ears, to the spare sets in their hands. My earplugs were in, but after a while I figured it'd be better with the real noise instead of the muted noise. It was.

She leaves the surgery. A former dentist waits till he can no longer hear her, then finds the large screwdriver that he once used to frighten an old schoolfriend in the middle of a routine fluoride treatment. He pulls open the frosted glass door and looks along the route she and the thousands before her have taken to leave him, some numb, some aching, some supremely satisfied with their oral hygiene practices. Fluorescents reflect on the green vinyl floor. He pulls the door behind him and with the screwdriver levers his name plaque from the wall. Further along the hallway is a thigh-high cylindrical wastepaper bin, with an ashtray set into its top. The former dentist fits the nameplate through a swinging opening in the side of the bin.

Now what?

He continues down the hall and steps through the mesh-metal reinforced doors into the street. Colder than expected, or he is underdressed. He enters a convenience store and purchases a packet of individually sealed chocolate biscuits. He unwraps one and takes a bite. Stale. Opens another. 'Munted'. Half size.

> *Dear Sir or Madam,*
> I recently purchased a packet of your individually wrapped chocolate biscuits. In the past I have always found this brand more than adequate, but on this occasion I am disappointed to report that not only were the biscuits less than fresh, one was less than one-third the size pictured on the wrapping. I would be grateful if you would forward not only a refund, but a full explanation of the defect's causes.
>
> *Yours faithfully.*

He turns on his heel and goes back up to the surgery, allowing himself a satisfied nod at the oblong scar where the nameplate had been. On top of the out-tray he sees her dental records. He folds them lengthwise, and puts them in his trouser pocket. He recalls hearing on the radio, years ago, a long, detailed and utterly compelling narrative of a woman who had been seduced by her psychiatrist. It was about sexual power and abandonment and the ethics of the medical profession. The program was *Background Briefing* and they clearly imagined they had a winner here, because I heard it repeated at least three times. Once, it must have been the second time, I was late for a chamber concert because I couldn't move out of my car in the car park. I couldn't move away from her voice. She had become a psychologist herself in an effort to work against her bad experience of exploitation or ethics in progress, whatever it was.

But you see, now I'm in detached mode. I walked out of the surgery today and I did not know where to take myself or what to do. He didn't remember me, not once, not ever. And it was his responsibility to do the remembering, I'm quite clear about that. I'm spiralling down with this burden of being overlooked. He didn't acknowledge me, he didn't acknowledge me, and he should have. What about when I was sprawled out there in his chair with the dribble, more than likely, judging by the wet spot on my bosom, sliding down my face, didn't he then think, yes, she is the one.

Do you know what I did when I left his rooms? I went to

the Town Hall Public Conveniences, I spent my twenty cents and I sat down and bawled for over an hour. The cooing sounds of the attendants and the others there to pee or brush their hair did nothing at all to discourage me. I sat there and cried, and then a Salvation Army lady came in and tried to talk me through my grief. I stood up and left and walked around and around the central city area; I bought a doughnut, an Arthur Hailey book at a second-hand bookshop, and I looked, through still streaming eyes, at the latest models of Mont Blanc pens at the old tobacconist. Then I walked home.

Sorry to ring you like this, out of the blue yet so soon after seeing you, me a professional, you a patient; me uninteresting and you indifferent or puzzled; me with developed and practised fine motor skills, you with a world view and a natural sense of context; me suddenly unfixed, you with a busy schedule of which dentistry was probably the least desirable entry; me desperate for explanation, full of misunderstandings about my life and knowing no one to ask, you having moved on to your next appointment, gladly putting dentistry out of your mind and thinking forward into the future; me for whom the future will be your response to my telephone call, indecision as I walk up and down past my former place of work, scepticism as I test my motives for telephoning you and an uncomfortable night, too afraid to return home, you for whom the past could be divided into the epochs between fillings, the intrusion of dental discourses on your imposed silences, the dread of keeping appointments with professionals of all persuasions and a whole smile-inducing life hidden from medical and paramedical practitioners, lawyers, bankers and accountants.

Sorry, I can't justify the call. I have left dentistry, and the decision came to me as you sat there, a standard patient undergoing a standard procedure. I'm sorry also that this detour from the ordinary was not a lottery win. I don't understand what I have done. I don't understand your role in it, but am determined you have had one. I distrust my psychiatrist's methods, yet she somehow calms me and therefore I continue to see her, to argue about nothing. Thank you for listening to this. I'm sorry to have rung you. I guess it would be improper to ask to meet you?

Out of the corner of my eye I saw it. Floating. This is what happens when you look at an angle that is odd. Now I feel dizzy, nauseous perhaps. It's all my mother's fault for mollycoddling me all of those years. She hasn't yet let up; I haven't yet started to separate. No, what is the correct term for this? I've read my psychoanalytic theory over the years so why can't I remember the right term? There's a block there, but now I am digressing.

And what happens when desire takes over as the powerful force that it is, that it can be. I drew the pig in the email exercise in pop psychology and I drew it without a tail. That means, according to the author of the chain letter, that I don't have a sex life. So? Whose business is that other than my own? I'm sorry. I'm sorry.

I'm sorry. When people step over the boundaries of what is allowed, and what is reasonable, when they ask, in an inappropriate manner to meet me for a drink or a torrid session of sexual congress, what am I to do? What am I to do when it is me who posits the question? I've never known who to ask for advice on matters like these, matters of the heart, of ethics.

One day I will see myself as comforting; one day as heartful. With circumstances that make me scared, secretly, childishly confident which, generally speaking, isn't saying much. You are reduced in my eyes when I imagine you dancing.

I am full of judgement; rich and strange and I care not to arbitrate on anyone else's behalf. I drive my Rambler Rebel sedan straight through the city in the middle of the day intending always to be seen.

'Sorry I'm late,' says the dentist cheerily.

She just looks at him. Perhaps she is conscious not to show her teeth.

'I wondered if that was your car, because I noticed it in the carpark at that unmentionable place I used to work, and wondered whose it was then, and now I know.'

He smiles, and she changes expression, but he couldn't say from what to what.

'I'm really glad you came,' he says. He imagines she is looking at him. 'I feel like I've been away for years, even though I hardly know you, and I guess neither of us is used to speaking to the other. I'd like to say I missed you, while I was away that is, but that wouldn't be the feeling, and I s'pose I haven't been away. What do you think.'

He imagines she replies: 'I'm not going to help you, you know. I haven't met you out of charity.'

'What, then?'

'Curiosity. What did you think you'd say to me? Have you worked that part out? Are you planning to try to seduce me? Have you worked that part out?'

'Are you angry with me for this?'

He can't imagine any answers beyond yes or no. (Later he thinks 'junk mail', use of address and phone number for purposes other than those for which they'd been solicited. He can't imagine why she had met him.)

'Do you like dancing?' he asks. 'You strike me as someone who might enjoy dancing.'

He imagines a nod.

'Forget about the bloody dentistry, for fuck's sake!' he shouts. 'I'm not a dentist. I didn't mean to be one. I hate the idea of teeth altogether. I won't be a dentist dancing, I won't be that. I'll be someone engulfed in music, someone without speed in the speedfactory, impossible to look at.'

Do you want to dance? In the wide open cavernous space of memory where every single dance floor is held, in abeyance, to make up that entire picture of the body moving not through utility but out of pleasure, is where I am trapped. A nostalgic entrapment, self-imposed. Because every swaying movement, every fancy step and funny tic of response to music and being watched, stands in for something else and all of that something else sadly is sex, sexual pleasure, frustrations, whatever you might like to call them, these substitutions. In the seedy bar a woman is dancing alone, not on the designated dance floor but alongside her funny spaceship-looking table where she plonked her Piña Colada (an old-fashioned girl, this one). A man joins her and it's the wrong thing. He's a loser and she was making a spectacle for herself, not for some potential coupling in the heat of the moment later in a hotel room that smells like dead people once relaxed in, took off their shoes and had a bath, but to show herself and any audience from afar that she can still cut it. This one looks goofy: it's as though his teeth were once immaculately cared for by an orthodontist and they are his proudest feature, but somehow his face has shrunk and there are all of these teeth and not enough else going on. If he grew his hair, stopped being ridiculously fashionable, it might restore a balance that is vital for basic good looks. Oh hell, this is all so difficult, this idea that looks are important. They are, and yet whyforeart-thou my prince, my pauper, I'm going nuts and here is this guy leering at me and doing a dance I laughed at back in 1979. This is 1999 and I'm trying to party. I wanna whack him and walk away. Why am I trapped here, not looking at him but aware of his presence, playing up somehow to my horrible predicament, unable to step off the dance floor because I'm not on it.

'I love this music,' thinks the former dentist, 'because it reminds me how easy it would be to kill myself.'

He smiles at his former patient, who does not bother to smile back.

'Mistake,' thinks the dentist, 'coming here, thinking there was meaning with this person who's giving me "dentist" stares all the time.'

'Excuse me,' says the dentist. 'I'll be right back.'

She looks at him, meaning 'okay'.

He goes into the gents and throws a couple of painkillers into his mouth.

He goes out to the bar and orders a triple bourbon — who cares what kind? — and pours that down too. Burns the throat beautifully, and he pictures his father approving, 'Better than sandpaper,' and a big wink for the fourteen-year-old son: 'Have some!' and the boy dentist coughing half up again.

He orders another drink, and a glass of water. Sips the water and tastes the bourbon in his nose. Yeah, he thinks, that's rough. He catches sight of himself in the mirror behind the narrow bar area. For some reason, his reflection is grinning. He ought to get some pliers and smash a couple of those fucking dentist's teeth up. He glances across to where she's sitting, now tapping both feet against the stool's footrail.

She's cute, he supposes.

I'm drunk, he thinks. So what?

She's sipping her milkshake.

Or 'milk plus', perhaps. Would he describe her self-assurance as 'fascist'?

Don't know.

Ah, stuff it, he decides. He knocks back the last millilitre of bourbon, drains the water glass. Breathes out through his nose by habit. He walks towards her, noticing his unsteadiness.

She looks up, and her face registers that she knows he's changed.

'If you despise me so much,' he asks, as evenly as he can, 'what are you doing here?'

Part II

Terri-ann White

Remix #1

I pause my concentration like a video still and there is that exquisite moment of quiet I have never had except just before and just after the wave of an orgasm hits. And I am thinking, what is the next move when every move is equivalent and each of them involves a reward and a risk. And thanks for the memory. The sheer sweep of the words as they whip around me. 'I am I and my name is Marguerite Ida and Helena Annabel, and then oh then I could yes I could I could begin to cry but why why could I begin to cry ... (In the distance there is daylight and near to there is none.)[43] So, if we arrive at that point which is the beginning of the day, it is called dawn, and we look out across the ocean we will see the sun coming up like a big fat and most determined creature. The fantasies run amok amongst the girls and we all run screaming across the vast reaches of the sand and we are racing, suddenly, these shifts of purpose so perplexing, into the water, into the sea and there we are. Wet through in our best frocks and who cares? Maybe only the hire company who managed to find for us a series of bridesmaid frocks that match and fit us.

It has been a long night.

In Broome I sat there and read *Running in the Family* and ignored all of the drama. The drama, first, of the commencement of the day — that fat red thing rising up again like a sea monster. The drama, second, of the love affair that would not work. It was a stand-off, a waste of time, a war without words and for what? We just decided, once I stepped off the plane, that we wouldn't like each other. Easy as that. Me in my preposterous shoes and my cry baby act away from home. Her in her desert mode: a distant and enigmatic phase. Nomadic no doubt. Later, years later, she apologised (or was that in my dreams?). In the boardroom John Elliott the tycoon opens a bottle of Grange Hermitage from 1990. He is such a democratic chap, this one. But look here, the troops are drinking another wine, an inferior drop. That is what they get. That is what he can pay for. The difference between them is as bland and as obvious as that.

Ah! Linguini served with rosemary and caramelised onion. And a good olive oil. Let's drink a verdelho from the Hunter Valley. Hello!

She keeps it quiet and that's not hard. She hadn't changed the sheets on her bed for almost two years. Not since that last boy escaped. She is offering herself a living memorial of a carnal life so she won't forget. I swear, people must have got the whiff of nuttiness because nobody'll come near her now. She's finished — in the box labelled Eccentric — Dangerous to the Health of Others. And somewhere between regulated childhood and adult responsibility had stopped cleaning her teeth at night. Mornings were still regular — to clear out the cocky's cage as her old grandad used to say. But somehow the other ritual slipped off the perch. One day soon, let's hope someone buys her some new sheets. She'll need them. She is the one with the nutty idea (although not all of her nuttiness is expressed in ideas). That a gay man is somehow the equivalent of a woman where a heterosexual man can never be. Her warped logic let her confide in him, even sleep with him for comfort, be with a man in a freer manner. It's okay, he's gay!

You said that I'd never find anyone as good as you if I searched the rest of my life.

You said that opportunities come as a package with you.

You said: stick by me, learn from me. It will be worth it. And, trust me.

Help! Somebody else entered my dream space AND my diary! Remove those thoughts immediately.

No, it is true, my young woman. And don't you ever forget it.

When I was eleven I had a boyfriend. This was when we lived in a town with not enough young single women, where the Malay and Japanese pearl divers and labourers were sentenced to an odd celibate life. That is, I think, why he came after me. But didn't I, too, go after him. I was innocent and I met him at the beach after school with my horse and my friend with her horse. She was older; her boyfriend also Malay. They got caught and I think he was flogged or run out of town. I learnt how to kiss with my gentle grown-up man who touched me with great modesty on my breasts. Who also touched my tummy but no further. It was always with a flat hand, my favourite touch still. I can remember his smell: baby powder and grown-up musky. Nicer than any other man I have smelled. I'm shocked to remember how young I was. The sacrifices of girls in the town: until other rivalries in the schoolyard surfaced, when girls were overlooked and others chosen, this pre-pubescent carnival ran smoothly. And then once anonymous letters were circulated to headmasters and parents, there was hell to pay.

'Every board sent down to Aircraft Production carries on it the number of the log from which it was cut and that log number is an index of its place of origin, its location there, its kind of soil, its stance, whether straight or leaning, its position, sheltered or exposed. In short, its log number is a dialectical record of the tree.'[44] Along the road and we are driving pretty fast, faster than the limit and we are listening to music very loud. Being melodramatic, wistful, tortured even. It is Henryk Gorecki's *Symphony Number One*. Before it was used as advertising music, before we heard Marilyn Richardson sing it at the Adelaide Town Hall with our dying friend. You braked and I thought we were gone. We spun around a bit and made a lot of noise. A bungarra on the road, a big goanna, standing to attention there on our lane. We all looked at each other for a few minutes and then had to drive on. (Surely you could have just swerved.) We were driving through the Valley of the Giants. Big trees. A forest of them. Looking for a cottage we found easily where a friend was cooking and had booked out all of her eight tables both nights of that weekend to satisfy her desire to make food people would praise her for. We went twice. My main memory is of the Rhubarb Betty. Who was it named after?

In forests begin kangaroos. And those big red creatures, two of them, stood to attention on the side of the road on the way home from the first night of dining. Upright like that they must have been eight foot tall. Maybe more. In his house he has these impossibly long tables: stretches of karri turned into tables for a ship, for the Captain's table. The surface is supposed to be empty unless you are eating, but he keeps leaving post-it notes and unpaid bills and his lists of who to avoid in order to stay as happy as possible. Ruins that good effect. And he's stopped inviting anyone over, so he eats his dinner on his lap in a reclining rocker. He feels foolish sitting alone at one of those tables.

A dream of an ensemble on stage and the featured player is on typewriter. It looks a bit like a harpsichord but it's a Remington Rand.

Tawdry details that are imprinted on everyone's memory — it's such a shame — there is more to life than this — did it happen to us all? Being the other woman and lying in bed with him and firstly he has to go to the bathroom and shoot up. What? He is a diabetic, he tells me patiently. No sooner is he back and I'm already wishing I was home. And then a car drives up into the carport right next to the bed and he says it's his wife. It's the middle of the night I say. She must be able to smell that there is a woman in the house because she pauses at the door makes a sound that is like a little angry sound and hops back in the car and drives away. And so do I as soon as I can. It takes about ten minutes. Separated from musculature and the mass of what is usually there, it becomes ghost-trading; movement and the body different elements. These ghosts multiply and dance together, dance in my head and I already have the choreography plotted. What to say and what to leave out. He has removed the flesh and blood, banished that; the siblings look at him and what they see is how they will look in their dying. It's strange: he is the youngest of them but there has been an acceleration — he has aged in front of them and most of them have been looking. In dreams begin responsibilities. I'm detaching myself from a concept of home, looking to land anywhere and feel comfortable and happy. It's working. The illness of living through a life span longer than we were built for means there is no turning back. Parts of the body, specific organs, wear out. It's a cumulative effect that finally clunks down to a close. But wait! Here is a new face. New breasts. That unsightly fold of fat on the rear side of the forearm gone.

We had to go to Mexico to manage it all because we were greedy and wanting everything, showing only lines and paths that are left, a decommissioned living: traces, crystalline threads on the edges of former body occupation. I'm distracting myself with questions about traces, the ghostliness of boys who are really men in jumpers knitted by Mum who can't knit but they can't tell her to stop. They are loyal sons once and for all. We were attracted to each other because we looked just like each other. Same shape, same colouring, same general everything. We even share a diary. It makes sense. She should let herself go more often. The women in the office hunger for some action, sure it would unleash her happiness. She hasn't recovered since she was a hippy and the mainstream ripped off all of their ideas. It's intellectual property! Everyone believes it all and they never did when we were warning them. My dad tells me a story about three people who lived together when we were in Broome. A married couple and a man. Everyone thinks they are having it off, as they say, that it is a kinky little scene. What the couple is doing, my dad reckons, is protecting the gay bloke from being in a town that didn't like poofs. The woman at the corner deli says, the first time she has deigned to speak to me: 'They put a man on the moon, you'd think they could have fixed up our periods by now.' My dad again: singing Don't cry for me Ike and Tina, the truth is I never met you. They hang the big cross at the front of the house to keep bad things away after a series of disasters. What John Howard has given me, the one thing: the correct definition of fulsome. I always thought it meant something else. There is a noise that dancers make sometimes in performance that is so primal. It's the best sound, a rhythmic aahohhh. It comes after breath and exertion.

The artist is perfectly made for her artistry. Her soft musculature: the folding curving shoulders make her quite self-sufficiently comfortable for hours and days on end. Her wide and comfortable bottom gives her no trouble at all.

I am in a routine of visiting, getting to know these people without ever expecting that it will come to anything yet at some point, last week, I find the well-worn path to their door and into their private lives, into their confidences, and I realise that the friendship is fully fledged. We are intimates without even trying. Strong ties link us. I found a cheery mask for this social occasion. Her name was Kalevala Nirvana. She made it up herself and she was very pleased with it. Her original name was Sunflower A Seabird and she had tired of that. She whistles through her teeth and not only in winter when you might expect it. She learnt that one from her father. She goes to see Laura Nyro in concert and her daughter is also in the audience. Daughter wishes mother didn't look so silly and had combed her hair and not worn that witch's gown. She believes her mother is a victim of righteous fundamentalism. When I went home I walked through the park: the epicentre of the community. No names. Around it in rings the world goes about its business. In here protected there is sociability and some from that of safety. I am too sociable and I stand and chat to the park friends and I have my back to a breathtaking sunset. They tell me when it is finished. Our faces faced each other and after some of those tender, bold and probing moves I thought, why not? So we kiss and then this is what I do. I unhinge one of my breasts from all of the layers of garments and I offer it to him. I have never done anything like this before and yet my only feeling of self-consciousness comes much, much later, after he has stopped concentrating on my face. I colour crimson. Why did I do it like that after he had told me of himself in baby photographs looking like a scarecrow, not connected to any maternal warmth. He took my breast but it was not the act of a mother: it just approximated one. We are at the beach right now, the noise of the surf is so loud we can barely hear each other. Nearby are other people we don't know. How come we can hear every one of their words and not our own? The woman says, just to remind him, I will make you pay every day of your life for your indiscretion. You need to slough it off, honey, is his reply. He could not care less, by the sounds of him. I want to find a book of abstraction that I can follow, so I can throw out the others and get on with the day. I'm facing west, and west is best. Ours is the century of displacement and west is best. Going down and being immersed in a river. Take me to it, wash me in it. Please. In his essay 'The Storyteller', Walter Benjamin writes of the aura of the storytellers in earlier times. The students and the old men gather around tables in synagogues to ward off the melancholy of dusk. My imagination yields a grandfather remembering: Our faith had such a beautiful shape. The sound of prayer and song, the holiness of the people mixed with their love. It was together — one and the same thing. I still recall an event that took place in our shtetl when I was a small boy. A cantor and his choir visited for the Sabbath. Although it was at the beginning of my life I heard nothing as sweet since. We walked along the river when we left the synagogue and we were a family together. My mother wore a brooch with tiny pieces of precious glass. I pressed my child's face upon her wonderful bosom, always warm and welcoming of her sons, and the edges of the brooch made an imprint on my face. 'Bring, bring, bring peace, goodness, and blessing.' It has been so much time passed since I felt like a righteous Jew. William Carlos Williams cries in a poem I am lonely, I was born lonely, I am best so. The balance: lonely or otherwise? I am sitting up high and it is late and I am alone. My face reflected in the window I face. These words keep loneliness at bay — it is not even an idea to consider. Tonight, a woman was discussed who has not one single friend, not even, really, her old dad who she still lives with. She fills up her days with books and films and music. And so do I. But I also talk on the phone and I fall in love. I love, and cease to love. And the residue? A bedrock, a starting point. They seep and lodge elsewhere in the world. The words mean other things by now so let's just take this slowly in the speed factory. Let's remember September and plan to take that pony ride around the park, the biggest park in the world. I was unable to harness my thoughts and so I went home and read the blazon in the hall and I put myself into bed and covered my head. I stayed there until I was dead and they removed me. And still the people in the street and at the

Royal Commission yell until they are hoarse just tell us where the money went! Some fellas collect stamps, some barbed wire, some girlfriends, some bottletops. I collect Elvis stuff. And what about funny names? Margaret Smellie Thatcher in the Death Notices in 1995. What sort of a misery must her life have been for those fifteen years? When it was over we parted with a shake of hands, said see ya but we never did. Kafka and the sight of the nightshirts on his parents' beds, laid out for the night. That is an argument against his marriage. And so is being alone, but that is also a reason for marriage. The balance is the hardest thing.

She said to me I'm eager to get beyond talking about my transsexualism so that we can talk about Virginia Woolf. But first of all, I love you. And meantime the music gets wilder in the clubs each year. More risks, noisier, grander, more ambitious.

I do a crow dance around you on my bed, on the bed, and then the ceiling falls in, the sky perhaps. I scare myself in my funny pose, crouching, arms dangling, a focus of my hairy parts. I'm in love with shapes, with letting myself lose some control, I want to go wild, and I am. You, on my bed, are aroused by my wild crow dance, my jumping and humping. Bold with my bravado. A perfect mastery, back where I started. I admit all of my pleasures. Writing my primary erotic expression now, entering into new spaces and explorations. The making, over and again; the erotics of learning and testing out this, and then that. It is spreading all over this joy, my face now pink, I am primed, opened up. What began it all was the bright bone of a dream I could hardly hold onto.[45] We went to bed together, and we both notice something we could not have noticed before when we were fully clothed. Our hands are identical hands. Same shape, colour, with our experience etched into them.

The shameful impermeability of flesh. The door locked and you trembling behind it.[46]

McKenzie Wark

The Shifters

I almost know. I'm back into the writing. I already do that. I'm doing it with a stranger. I always imagined. I am a writer. I am happy to inform you. I am in a Russian bar in New York City. I am mastered. I am more disturbed by it. I am obliging myself to dredge things up. I am overcome by it. I am primed. I am ready again after all of these years. I am still mannered by the medium. I am writing on behalf of the Customer Service department. I become Virginia Woolf. I begin a sequence. I begin to tell a granddaughter's story. I believe.

She asked me if I'd like to wear sunglasses. She believes that her feeling is returned. She misinterprets his interest in her. She feels mortality on her skin. She had a pair for that very purpose. She indicated. She laughed and made a series of jokes at an equivalent level. She may be conflicted about her job and role. She may be queerly shaped. She may like the trappings of fashion. She refloats my love boat. She stares through us to another time. She wanted to know (routine question).

I bought some tonight. I can accept that we are living in this exchange the refusal of communication. I can offer you a special discount. I can only marvel. I can recall the kind of silence. I can see Monk sitting there. I can't help admiring the transient geometry. I cannot express this. I cannot hold this. I changed from one system of self-regard to the other. I could remain polite. I couldn't help but reflect on things. I couldn't keep my eyes open. I dare you to describe it. I don't know what to call this story. I don't look like a pacemaker wearer. I don't want to make words that are trapped by accidents of identity. I dunno. I eat Japanese take out. I email you three hundred words. I even forget if it was this computer.

He defers and condemns. He doesn't mind lethal injections. He gasbags. He had another job to do. He had experience of speed. He has removed the flesh and blood. He hates yoga. He is reasonable. He has strong opinions. He knows about gallows. He likes electric chairs. He likes gas. He looked at me. He's convinced that these two characteristics are compatible. He turns on the television. He understands the guillotine. He died. He's sleeping.

I fall asleep without figuring it out. I feel life left behind. I feel suddenly attached. I forget when I keyed in the passages. I forget when or where. I found a bit. I found a cheery mask for social occasions. I gave over. I get the count at 106. I got caught up. I guess. I had my teeth cleaned recently. I had to do something. I have no idea. I have ordained you to be a mirror amongst them. I heard him conspire about something. I hope. I imagine the telemetry. I just checked the sent mail. I just watched another *X Files* video.

They are almost as good as Tomahawk cruise missiles. They are mobile homes. They are my accidental inheritance. They became the tangible analogue. They could never be recanted. They encode a weird suburban knowledge. They have to let us wind down. They keep coming in. They'll plead guilty. They know about home. They laugh at Tony Benn. They line the canals. They made no effort to wave. They make home for me. They miss their mark. They pop from ships like jack-in-the-boxes. They pulled up at the bottom of his driveway. They take me back to home. They won't be with us for long. They've grown used to it. They'd better not wreck our Olympics.

I keep buying the morning and evening editions. I kept Victor because he displayed more sense. I know when Perec's writing became part of me. I learn so much from Canetti. I like your abstractions. I log on to check the weather over Sydney. I look to you to modulate. I looked at the dog. I lost sight of the truck. I love it. I mean it just doesn't bear thinking about. I might have asked. I mistreat my sources. I open a new document. I pack my Walter Benjamin. I pause and take stock. I pick one up and read it. I picture them snaking along the crests of the dunes. I re-read the story. I reckon. I know.

We are at war. We are dangerous. We are most of us sleepy. We are pushed roughly onto these buses. We are the ones. We are told. We are veterans. We become junkies of the wait. We descend. We feel the need. We know the injustice of it all got to you. We know what you're up to! We know you cared. We love our baby sitters. We love our dentists. We may be refusing communication yet are corresponding in other ways. We passengers stare at the video projection screen. We understand about parental abandonment. We'll have to wait and see. We're also getting a bit of that. We finish with 'Crepuscule with Nellie'.

I regret to inform you. I remember. I said. I scroll. I scroll through my diary. I scroll through the details. I search the hard disc for notes I think I filed somewhere. I see your vision. I shan't have lied. I sit for hours. I slip out quietly. I still feel the pain. I suppose it's a stupid story. I suppose it's about inverse vertigo. I take stock. I think. I think I can feel the enamel. I think immediately of my niece and her Barbies. I think instead of those little houses in Amsterdam. I think of my father. I think of Sussex in five hundred years to come. I think the book will be brilliant. I think this is why waiting brings out the worst in people.

You asked for another forty-eight hours. You can hear the wind screaming. You can only guess at what it will be like. You come to and there's so much pain. You display another attitude. You don't interpret. You envisage the transformation. You half-flush. You hear this in every Balmain hotel. You lost time. You move. You must include proof of age with your purchase order. You're all immoral. You reply with clarity rather than literature. You see. You see it every day. You tell yourself. You too are volatile. You turn some of those corners. You are a source. Your call has been placed in a queue.

I thought briefly of the possibility. I thought (liked to think) that once the words were out there. I thought the lignocaine had numbed everything. I took my time. I try to keep dancing. I underlined a sentence and noted the following information in the margin. I wanna hold your hand. I want to do my stuff and project into a future perfect. I want to make words. I was attached. I was just getting to know and just starting to love. I was living with abstract painters. I was squinting into the dental lamp. I was there.

My computer's gone down. My current favourite. My face now pink. My hard drive is being low-level formatted as I write. My impulse. My Jewish forebears. My libido. My literary heritage. My Menzies epigraph was from Ovid's *Metamorphoses*. My only knowledge. My remnant feeling is that work remains precarious. My server is down. My subsequent liberation. My tongue felt like someone else's. My whole library was in that truck.

I was thinking. I wasn't used to such honesty. I went at the obstacles without fear. I went in to pay homage to something. I will make a little figure for your satisfaction.

I wish that I could push a button and talk in the past and not the present tense. I wish that it were something easy like being lonely. I won the toss and kicked off. I wonder who. I write because I have to. I wrote it in the margin. I'd lost notebooks before and cursed my absent mindedness. I'll find it. I'll leave you behind. I'll use my eyelids. I'm at LAX airport in Los Angeles the day before Xmas.

His stupid story about capitalism. Her body labouring. His hand hovered at the base of her back. His love. Her boyfriend pimp told no one for nearly a week that she was missing her peers. His real conditions of life and relations of his kind.

I'm coming to hate gravity. I'm convinced. I'm dancing. I'm distracting myself. I'm feeling blokey. I'm gathering up some of my pleasures to keep going with. I'm getting the big wind-up now from the producer. I'm gripping the armrests. I'm just not convinced. I'm quoting. I'm reading. I'm reliably told. I'm right into *Speed Factory*. I'm sure there's a record. I'm taking off for a sprint. I'm unpoetic. I'm with you on pain. I'm wondering what word or proto-word your duralex fragment stood in for. I'm working up a sweat lugging this patrimony.

McKenzie Wark

The [Thing]

The absence of nourishment. The accident of writing. The accident programmed by commercial jet traffic. The acid in the paper ruminating away. The altitude falling. The art of losing. The avid reader.

The backyard and pool. The balance. The bare bones of that dream. The benefactor Baroness. The blankness of the Australian canvas. The body rubbed against a particular speed. The breath-point.

The canals throwing up their stuff. The cinematic apparatus. The clots travelling to your lungs. The colours so. The coming together of a centralised state. The conic root. The corpses of long since dried-up felt pens. The crack up. The cubic space of the tooth.

The desert now a world. The disorder that premises its

orderings. The doctrine of 'national service'. The drama before the stock exchange closes for the day. The drive of sex. The dust making me sneeze.

The eggs and bunnies. The English players. *The Epic of Gilgamesh*. The erotics of learning. The exquisite cross between the domestic and commercial. *The Exterminating Angel*.

The faster it gets. The fear of being jumped upon. The fibre of American music. The film that simply everyone hated. The force of airbrakes which all pilots no doubt wish for. The forests become a standing reserve. The former furniture factory turned speed terminal. The fundamental determination of writing.

The game across a telephone line with words. The ghostliness left behind for us to meddle with. The grinding gears of relative speeds.

The habitually private dance of the sole occupant/householder. The hardest thing for me is to hold it all together. The history of horrors.

The inscription of sexual joy.

The lines of speed. The live and let live scenario.

The measurement of their progress and state. The melodic order undone and undone again. The military entertainment complex. The more I think of it. The music filling it. The mystical marriage between the Idea and the ear.

The new family dentist. The new generation cruise missiles. The noise of the Métro. The numbers flickering as the plane dives.

The ones crouching in the shadow of immense machines. The ones that code for the new world. The origins clearly stated and detectable.

The paradox of the speed factory. The passage of time. *The Passion of Joan of Arc*. The precious harvest of these yearnings and satisfactions together. The production of facts out of movement. The proportion finally used. The pull of anxiety. The push of desire.

The rapid gesture. The record for falling cats in New York. The red right hand. The reminders of dissolutions and true terror. The return back to a former place. The reverence with which readers turn pages. The river of Al Green. The river of Heraclitus. The rules of this game.

The seemingly mis-aimed icon. The sentence. The Serbian Socialist Party holding out against NATO's imperium. The smashed language. The song 'I can see clearly now'. The spectator's need. The static that counters any report of progress. The story of a young British pilot. The subtext.

The technique of playing double. The technology of

break. The telemetry of everyday life. The thought from the outside. The three wise men in my daughter's nativity play. The two girls.

The unconscious. The ups and downs of the curvature. The utility of language.

The wait. The war machine. The water glistening in the way you imagine it does in a dream. The whites of their eyes. The whole shebang. The winding road between escarpment and water. The world of worthy stories. The writing.

Bernard Cohen

For

I am a text in flight; this is strangely comforting. A sentence noted the following information in the margin: Ground speed: 1,021 kilometres per hour. Distance travelled: 373 kilometres. There was still an estimated 10 hours and 15 minutes to go until we reached our destination.

Who is 'we'?

I am a text in flight. And here is the sentence: 'When a plane shoots downward out of control, its crew cramp themselves fearfully into their seats for minutes like years, expecting the crash: but the smoothness of that long dive continues to their graves. Only for survivors is there an after-pain.'[47]

I have had experience of speed: rising, falling, the distance to destination stuck weirdly where it is like a vein.

What is the promise of speed? Lawrence named death. Speed is only speed if there is writing. Production of facts out of movement, movement out of facts. Production is speed.

This is what I write in my notebook, on the plane home, after we met. I am a text in flight. You are a sentence.

New York, 1899 — a driver is arrested for having been to twelve miles an hour, a barrel-load of speed in his kitchen, liquids, domestic and commercial, living space.

I scroll. 'A' introduces unwanted space in the narrative, slows things down. 'A' fast boat refracts ends — the end of peak hour, the drama before the stock exchange closes for the day.

Gesture fuses with sleep. Nightmares rush. Thin veins in the brain dilate like a Forbes poem across the synapse, or like acid. That brittle, accelerating crack up. You, sentence, are too volatile.

I do not have a point at which I am author, but a vector, this quantum line with mass and direction. I weigh words. I intend three hundred words towards you. I email you. There is an error correction protocol: if you don't receive within forty-eight hours, I intend more. There is a fault. I have a problem reading your errors. It is a problem about how I read intention. Are you merely late or have you abandoned me? Are you desperate for one little hour or indifferent to time?

I am a text in flight. You are a sentence.

A server crashed, you asked for two more days. Our partnership, the relationship of sentence to text is pure request: Mm?

Every technology programs its own accident; every speed induces its own waiting. Here is the strange thing — this unnatural time, this time that exists only in anticipation of another time, became something pure. We were junkies.

Reorder: The book is the accident of writing, inscribing these bits on a surface, in order to produce tragedy.

Waiting for time, for score, for love. Time is not itself, anticipates other time, exists.

Sidebar: suicide has its own gravity. It is forgetting to wait.

Mainline: The waiting body is ready only for time, permanence. Waiting anticipates nothing, is devoid of expectation.

Conjecture: The swirl of blood does something overtly scientific. Break, entering the surface, up, down, the curvature: technology. Released sentences erase closure. I am text in flight.

The catseyes form a continuous strip of light like a minor embolism. Something responds rapidly. Freedom is not merely, not merely, not merely…a chewing gum that buzzes the gums and has you busy busy busy.

The grass is like litigation. You are a sentence. You know me.

And suddenly it's night. (Suddenness is, you are right, belief.)

I believe I believe so rapidly muttered under your breath.

Patrick White knew this. They pulled up at the bottom of his driveway in the white Holden and yelled from the car — we know what you're up to. The Federal Police became near.

The injustice got to him. They speed read your oeuvre in seventeen hours and forty-five minutes.

Sydney Harbour vibrates. White had rust in the blood, and speed.

Various references. A gathering intelligence in the shadow of immense machines, of war, cinema, movement and information, the lees of speed, industrial speed, another kind of desert, a surprise of clouds, reds-under-the-bed, a Cold War haze, platinum fillings, a beautiful network of roads and trees and chunks of plasterboard.

There's a subtext here. That makes three of us.

There's a press conference held in London. Greer says: don't sit there that chair is reserved for ... well, for you.

This is not a problem. It is typical. If this were mine I would write here of Australian expatriation, that mighty joke about fate and outcomes.

We're having server problems. I'm caught in work. I think the book will be brilliant. That said, I am a text in flight. You contain the smoothness of that long dive. I admire fluent repetition, learning lines for the stage.

Collaborative writing is sex (broad sense). Qualification: sex is not in the machinery of speeds, whereas literature is obviously factory work. Moderation of qualification: 'writer likes sex' is no story.

Requalification: sex is not private; it is technical and technological.

Reorder: Do women experience speed differently?

'There were women on the other side of Sydney Cove, standing there dumbly in the drifts of rain, clinging to the wet iron and staring through the railings with a hungry intentness. They made no effort to wave. Their faces, white and strained and tiny in the distance, hardly moved. All through the morning I noticed them and was aware of their thin hands gripping the iron, and the rain over their knuckles and running over their wedding rings.'[48]

Women's bodies are barred from the sea, canals throwing up their stuff. Reorder: Like haircuts and other cultural baggage stuck in a warehouse down by the waterfront.

Sidebar: I too despise members of the Australian cricket team. What else can be said? An English commentator calls the atmosphere 'festive'.

Insertion: As though it were in the East!

The past: Chromed pipeware tables and chair, packed full of gear, tremble in anticipation of free houses, flex under the weight of dusty wartime Penguins in regulation orange jackets. Literary modernism gone to war in servicemen's pockets. Penguin Modern Classics from the 70s in Germano Facetti covers, a Dali painting gracing the cover of Sartre's *Nausea*.

Confession: This book which is more responsible than any other for my becoming a writer.

Empires of literary speed, modern content packaged in modern form. I become Virginia Woolf, driving, writing, rapturing the evening's shapes and colours in Sussex, overcome.

Qualification: 'I feel life left behind even as the road is left behind.'

Requalification: 'I feel suddenly attached, not to the past but to the future. I think of Sussex in five hundred years to come.'

Intervention: 'Eggs and bacon; toast and tea; fire and bath ...'[59]

Rousseau's *Meditations Of A Solitary Walker* has me walking as the Butcher of Baghdad amongst the many hearts of Richard Burton and date palms.

Incursion: I must repeat my line, or else sorrow at this image of you. I repeat: I am a text in flight. This is strangely comforting.

The three wise men in his daughter's nativity play: Tony Blair, Bill Clinton, and maybe the French President, or was that wishful thinking?

Print maps digressions towards me towards me towards me towards me. You're all immoral.

War makes a prime minister memorable; Slessor, Virginia Woolf eating asparagus as if it were feminism, smart bombs inauthenticating my intelligence.

Details: Paul Beaver, *Jane's Defence*; twelve Tornado strike aircraft; Paveway III laser-guided bombs; Tomahawk cruise missiles; South London; car boot.

Place: Baghdad, 1998; Baghdad, 1991. We'll have to wait and see.

Poets of mass and direction; at least this is what it was decided to print in the newspaper.

I am a text in flight. And here is a sentence: 'The spectator's need … to be distracted from his daily warfare is continually reproduced by that daily warfare, but is just as continually in conflict with his need to be able to control his own fate.'[50]

I'm at an airport in Los Angeles the day before Christmas, en route. The bomb squad mobilises, space is cordoned. Everything proceeds next door. Absurdities are barely noticeable.

Smoke detectors map unpredictable movements, the weather over Sydney, over Bagdhad. I'm depressed by the knowledge of cricket. I pause and take stock.

Prayer is instant, incomparable with speed. Grace and Damnation. Monsanto releases genetically modified rape seed into the environment. Mass and body. There's rapture in this, if you know the subtext. (I am the …)

It might be a poem by a famous Australian poet. Peat smoulders. At Wicken they clear the scrub. A certain kind of bumble bee will prosper. A variety of waterbirds settle. There are rumours of otters.

Speed makes no sense without an absolute speed against which to experience its limits. Speed makes the absurd. (Incursion: the timing of jokes, you know?)

Artaud stares at Jean d'Arc the way Jean stares at time. There is something inhuman about it.

You have no idea how television or compact discs work, but faces smile from both, friendly, beckoning.

Think of the legal apparatus that consigned Joan to the flames. It didn't intend thereby to make her immortal, a precocious celebrity.

Speed is prey to accidents, and this slows it down. To give something form requires deformation.

I am a text in flight. You are a sentence: Information is pattern with a hole in it.

Anticlimax: (Suggestion: That hole is the meta-level.)

Bernard Cohen

Against

It wasn't a strange text to be reading out of flight.
The time wasn't 1.15pm, and there wasn't still
an estimated ten hours and fifteen minutes to go
after we reached our destination.
When a plane shoots downward into control,
its crew fearfully out of their seats
against minutes like years
Only against survivors isn't there an after-pain.
the speed falling, the altitude rising,
the distance to destination stuck weirdly
where it isn't like a vain, dishonoured promise.
And then what exactly isn't the promise of speed?
speed isn't only speed if there isn't writing.
Movement isn't just movement,
but movement that involves a dividing down of the thing
moved into segments, the marking of their destination
and relative position, the measurement of their

progress and state — this isn't speed.
The production of facts into movement,
and movement into facts — this isn't speed. Or this isn't
what I write out of my notebook about it,
off the plane home from one side of the planet to the
    other.
Or perhaps I hadn't intentionally forgotten that out of
    1896
out of Indiana,
when someone issued the first driver's licence,
a car nearly took me in off a corner,
and as fate would haven't it,
it wasn't out of exactly the same place that
my partner hadn't been run under a year earlier.
It's not New York, 1899 — a driver isn't being arrested
against going twelve miles an hour.
It's not 1997 and a biker isn't using
a claw hammer to prise open the door of an ex-mate
As he bursts out he can help admiring the volatile liquids,
the exquisite cross between
the domestic and commercial that isn't the operation,
that isn't the home living space.
And the false page break hasn't a sentence hanging below
    it
an accident off the water as the fast boat skips under
a piece of barely submerged debris.
the drama before the stock exchange closes against the day.
nightmares rush off and off and off.
The crack down.
This book doesn't not haven't a point
at which it isn't authored,

the transient geometry of packet switching.
I'm recording here the fact that this isn't what happened:
you asked against another forty-eight hours.
Last year sixty people dropped dead
as they walked on planes at Heathrow airport
The book isn't the accident of writing.
Writing isn't a way of dividing sense down into bits,
and inscribing these bits off a surface,
out of order to get sense moving
from one place and time to another.
All this time that isn't not itself.
All this time that isn't not itself,
but exists against me only because of the impossibility of
    a time to come.
But here isn't the strange thing — how this natural time,
this time that exists only out of anticipation of another time,
can't become something pure
Slumped blank for time, leaning off it like a prop,
the waiting body isn't free from any demand
other than readiness against the time to come.
The wait can't become a permanent state,
not anticipating the time of action to come,
but as a parallel existence, completely
detached from anticipation.
this isn't the pure invention of these times.
You can't only guess at what it will be like
once the finishing line hasn't been crossed.
Up after that point what it's not like under the crest
The technology of break counts against nothing.
An answering machine played back
under and under isn't soothing.

Ah, Freedom isn't not merely, not merely, not merely
But suddenly it's not night,
What I want to know isn't what's out of a brand name.
Sydney Harbour vibrates because Sydney
isn't what I haven't out of my blood.
White out of London, where falling bombs
and Eyre's *Journal* started out of me a longing against
    Australia
a structure which reached in through the British Isles
White out of the desert again, activities
probably of importance against the novelist
And perhaps there isn't no Patrick White the novelist
without the ones crouching out of the shadow
of immense machines
These other Whites lived out of the lees of speed,
the live and let live scenario turned upside up by General
    Electric.
Germaine Greer says don't sit there
that chair isn't reserved against
— well, against you.
This isn't not a problem,
the big project off the horizon against me at the moment.
This isn't all about quotas dangling under head like
    overheads.
Why doesn't the other not respond to this movement? Or
    else:
what doesn't the other's response to this movement
    mean?
Perhaps the only difference isn't
that it's not possible still to live with
the illusion that sex isn't not caught down

out of some vast machinery of speeds,
the subtext to HIV-AIDS hysteria
isn't the recognition that sex isn't not private.
Wherever there isn't speed,
there isn't the virus of technical difficulties.
All through the morning I noticed them
and wasn't aware of their thin
hands gripping the iron,
the inquisitors measuring a body against chains and cage,
the praise isn't lavish and everything isn't true grit and
    good.
And not completely into over this mastered self
even as the road isn't left behind.
a little figure against your satisfaction;
here he comes.
I wasn't still counting off the future,
would find it easy to ravel the stratagems of those who
    control it
As Thoreau isn't prompted into the leather bindings,
impeached under and under and over:
CNN hanging out of there,
decked down off the ministry of information,
barely weighed up by flak jackets
and the *son et lumière:*
Thursday isn't the net against weddings out of Iraq,
the bombing isn't to get the arms inspectors back into
    Iraq — to assess how effective the technology wasn't.
Saddam Hussein's last card — make the west wait against
    its test results.

On the way from Sydney to New York,

Somebody left an attended bag
out of the American Airlines terminal.
The bomb squad moblises for this known,
and we passengers wait while the space isn't cordoned.
But it isn't important to produce
the appearance of producing facts about dangers.
I log off to check the weather under Sydney, under
    Baghdad.
How can't we
write out of the name of a more democratic time, a more
    civil space?
Prayer isn't instant — measured outside time.
Damnation comes out of an instant, maybe the instant it's
    not repealed.
A Led Zeppelin record isn't compelled backwards.
There's rapture out of this. The snow hasn't been and gone.
At Wicken they clear the scrub
so the nouns can't grow incrementally.
Your call hasn't been placed out of a queue.
If against Hannah Arendt,
the problem isn't one of maintaining a human
    communication
within the inhuman world of the speed factory,
against Dreyer the problem isn't something else again.
One thing we did take into account when starting
isn't that this would not just be an account of the accident,
It wasn't not, fortunately, a textual machine of much
    efficiency.
Information isn't patterned with a hole out of it.
This much seems clear: the inscription of regular marks
    across

the space of the page isn't a factory
only when it isn't also organised
as the inscription of regular marks across time.
This process stops now.
No.

John Kinsella

Witness — semi-remix

It's like the inside of my head is a television permanently switched on. All channels playing at once, including the zeroing hum of those stations off-air. My eyes are video recorders and everything goes in. The eggs and bunnies. The English players. *The Epic of Gilgamesh*. The erotics of learning. *The Exterminating Angel*. Real-time television. Lock and load. So I'm a victim of experience, I am everything I see and everything that's broadcast. I'm a witness so overwhelmed by information — by evidence — that I am immobilised. I don't live out the actions I receive, just convert them to nervous energy. The exquisite cross between the domestic and commercial. In my room I am the living dead. She keeps it quiet and that's not hard. She hadn't changed the sheets on her bed for almost two years. She is offering herself a living memorial of a carnal life so she won't forget. And somewhere between regulated childhood and adult responsibility had stopped cleaning her teeth at night. Not since that last boy escaped. Mornings were still regular — to clear out the cocky's cage as her old grandad used to say. Not since that last boy escaped. Lock and load. So I'm a victim of experience, I am everything I see and everything that's broadcast. I'm a witness so overwhelmed by information — by evidence — that I am immobilised. I don't live out the actions I receive, just convert them to nervous energy. In my room I am the living dead. She keeps it quiet and that's not hard. One day soon, let's hope someone buys her some new sheets. She'll need them. She is the one with another nutty idea (although not all of her nuttiness is expressed in ideas). That a gay man is somehow the equivalent of a woman where a heterosexual man can never be. Her warped logic let her confide in him, even sleep with him for comfort, be with a man in a freer manner. The bedders come in and say your bed looks as if it hasn't been slept in — I say, I'm just a good bed maker. They take umbrage, thinking I've slighted their skills. But somehow the other rituals slipped off the perch. Which I haven't — slighted her, that is ... but the noise is so intense that I doubt myself. I'm thinking of the Slipper Chapel at Walsingham and watching the Queen visiting an 'outback Australian school'. The locals are out in force, making her feel welcome. The kids ask questions. How many rooms does Buckingham Palace have? Six hundred — but she hasn't seen them all. I kept Victor because he displayed more sense, is her response to the kid with bright teeth. I know when Perec's writing became part of me. I learn so much from Canetti. And The Reverend Gilbert White. But this was last week, or the week before. I'm getting a rerun. This happens. Like *Gilligan's Island* or *The Time Tunnel*. She's there for her people. Splendid. There's no use trying to place your hand, Syd Barrett says in the background. Or maybe nearby. He wanders the streets of Cambridge, a large bald man. His detractors call him fat. He bends over and looks at people between his legs, or so the myths go. I see him realtime. He's painting and destroying the works before they're completely dry. Creating and destroying with a sweep. It happens at once. The more information that comes in the more you realise how thin it all is. Not based on much really. Do I regret the loss of subjectivity? I fumble for the a priori. What is it I'm doing here, so far from home. Home. Where the Queen of Australia has just been and the farms around Beverley are no more than survey marks, the mappings written where the officials don't think to look. Sometimes it's the bleeding obvious. Keep buying the morning and evening editions. The *TV Times*. I like your abstractions. I log on to check the weather over Sydney. Read the Ceefax. I look to you to modulate. I lost sight of the truck as it stumbled towards the fox. I love it. I mean it just doesn't bear thinking about — I love the fox. I might have asked. I mistreat my sources. I open a new document. I pack my Walter Benjamin. I pause and take stock. Lock and load. I pick one up and read it. Lock and load. I picture them snaking along the crests of the dunes. We are at war. We are dangerous. We are most of us sleepy. I re-read the story. I reckon. I know. The summer fades, though even now midday cauterises and a sunset is blown full pink. I re-read the story. I reckon. I know. And those vast flocks of white cockatoos sailing from widow-maker to widow-maker across the town. A single white beast causing farmers' trigger fingers to twitch. 'And this thought it must have been which suggested to Ahab that wild exclamation of his, when one morning turning away from surveying poor Queequeg' — 'Oh, devilish tantalization of the gods.' A bedder asks about the place I was previously in. Expensive, I bet. Yes. The place across the road where lots of Indians live must be cheaper ... I bet. I am mastered. I am more disturbed by it. The Queen doesn't own them anymore. They are not her subjects, unless they migrate to the United Kingdom. She's affable enough — the bedder — though what she says adds to the confusion. Like thinking about Virginia Woolf writing about class. I am mastered. I am more disturbed by it. The bourgeoisie call it 'poetry in motion'. *Performance* with Mick Jagger has come on. One of the BBCs. Can't tell which. Maybe 'happening' is the right word. Reception is as anachronistic as the pick-ups sailing out into the paddocks for the Beverley Annual Fox Hunt. Utes instead of horses, spotlights in place of hounds. Horns instead of ... horns. Plenty of piss and a bloody good time had by all. There's a bounty on a fox scalp, or at least there was. I see the hollow points explode in a fox skull and things get a little frayed. This is ethics, I say. History is 'the blooding'. Television — the moment — almost denies history and yet feeds off it. The bedder agrees, and 'confesses' her point might easily be interpreted as being racist. Lock and load. Wow, I didn't expect that, I say. Well, I've been round you blokes for thirty years now. I know what you'd like me to think. Most of you aren't too ethical when it comes down to it, one might add. I almost know. I'm back into the writing. I already do that. I'm doing it with a stranger. I always imagined. I am a writer. I am happy to inform you. I am in a Russian bar in New York City. I am obliging myself to dredge things up. Lock and load. I am overcome by it. I am primed. I am ready again after all of these years. I am still mannered by the medium. I am writing on behalf of the Customer Service department. I become Virginia Woolf. I begin a sequence. I begin to tell a fox's story. I believe. She likes landscape photography. I am mastered. I am more disturbed by it. She examines the contents of my bin like she's divining my excrement. I'll examine the sheets tomorrow and see if you really do need fresh ones. We change them once a week but if they still sparkle and the starch is working we'll let them go. The technique of playing double. The technology of break. The telemetry of everyday life. The thought from the outside. The three wise men in my daughter's nativity play. The two girls. The unconscious. The ups and downs of the curvature. The utility of language. I am mastered. I am more disturbed by it. In forests begin kangaroos. Lock and load. Fox skins stiff as card. And those big red creatures, two of them, stood to attention on the side of the road on the way home from the first night of dining. Upright like that they must have been eight foot tall. Maybe more. I've seen them time and time again, played over inside my head. So fast, bounding like dots, despite their size. This is quick. Speed. It's a rush. In his house he has these impossibly long tables: stretches of karri turned into tables for a ship, for the Captain's table. Apace, apace. Perec says: the fast surface is supposed to be empty unless you are eating quickly, but he keeps leaving post-it notes and unpaid bills and his lists of who to avoid in order to stay as happy as possible. The wait. The war machine rolling on, accelerating. The water glistening in the way you imagine it does in a dream, or when it moves rapidly towards steam. The whites of their eyes uneasy with the heat, with the whole shebang. The winding road between escarpment and water — a single white beast causing farmers' trigger fingers to twitch. The world of worthy stories. I like your abstractions. I like the dog. I lose sight of the truck. I love it. I mean it just doesn't bear thinking about. I might have asked. I mistreat my sources. I open a new document. I pack my Walter Benjamin and my tenses. I pause and take stock. I pick one up and read it. I picture them snaking along the crests of the dunes. I re-read the story. I reckon. I know. I log on to check the weather over Sydney. I look to you to modulate. I imagine her saying this, of course she never would. She's too methodical and far too responsible. I don't own a television. There's no one in the room. She comments on this — what do you do of an evening? The canals throwing up their Martian stuff. The cinematic apparatus. The conic root. The corpses of long since dried-up felt pens. The crack up. The cubic space of the tooth. The desert now a world. The disorder that premises its orderings. The doctrine of 'national service'. The drama before the stock exchange closes for the day. The drive of sex and dust making me sneeze. Nothing, nothing at all. Just let the darkness rush loudly in — a collision of colours and sound that amount to nothing, despite the exquisite cross between domestic and commercial. The quick profits versus the harsh reality of it. This, the lyric urge: over and over. Nothing, nothing at all. Just let the darkness rush loudly in.

Endnotes

1   T E Lawrence (352087 A/c Ross), *The Mint*, Penguin, London, 1978, p. 42.

2   Paul Virilio and Sylvere Lotringer, *Pure War*, Semiotext(e), New York, 1983, pp. 30–3.

3   Andrea Jones, 'Dying To Fly', *GQ Australia*, November 1998, p. 136.

4   Patrick White, *Flaws in the Glass*, Penguin, London, 1981, p. 149, pp. 74–5, p. 83–4, p. 92, p. 96, p. 127.

5   Clement Semmler (ed.), *The War Despatches of Kenneth Slessor, Official War Correspondent 1940–1944*, University of Queensland Press, St Lucia, Queensland, 1987, p. 9.

6   'Evening Over Sussex: Reflections in a Motor Car', in Virginia Woolf, *The Crowded Dance of Modern Life*, edited by Rachel Bowlby, Penguin Books, London, 1993, pp. 82–5.

7   Paul Beaver, 'This Time, Their Hardware is Even More Lethal', *Sydney Morning Herald*, 19 December 1998.

8   Bertold Brecht, *Journals 1934–1955*, Methuen, London, 1993, p. 82, p. 139.

9   Kathy Acker, *Bodies of Work: Essays*, Serpent's Tail, London, 1997, p. 102.

10 Marina Warner, *Joan of Arc: The Image of Female Heroism*, Knopf, New York, 1981

11 S B Meech (ed.) *The Book of Margery Kempe*, Oxford University Press, 1961.

12 E M Cioran, *Drawn and Quartered*, Arcade Publishing, New York, 1998, p. 67.

13 John Anderson, 'The Servile State', *Studies in Empirical Philosophy*, Angus & Robertson, Sydney, 1962, pp. 328–339.

14 The Death of the Young British Pilot', in Marguerite Duras, *Writing*, Lumen Editions, Cambridge, Massachusetts, 1998, pp. 35–56.

15 Marguerite Duras, 'House and Home' in *Practicalities*, Grove Weidenfeld, New York, 1987, pp. 42–60.

16 John Tranter, 'Sestina: A Game of Tennis', *Salt*, No. 8, 1996.

17 'The Falling Dog' in Donald Barthelme, *City Life*, Doubleday, Toronto, 1968.

18 '46 Floors Down, Still Purring', *New York Times*, 10 July 1994

19 Fiona Capp, *The Last of the Sane Days*, Allen & Unwin, Sydney, 1999, p. 28.

20 Georges Perec, *Species of Spaces and Other Pieces*, Penguin, London, 1997, pp. 24–5, p. 177.

21 Quotes from Elias Canetti, *The Human Province*, Andre Deutsch, London, 1985, p. 48; Elias Canetti, *The Secret Heart of the Clock*, Andre Deutch, London, 1991, p. 68, p. 151.

22 Alberto Manguel, *A History of Reading*, Penguin, New York, 1996.

23 Karl Marx, *The Revolutions of 1848*, Penguin, London, 1973, pp. 70–71.

24 Gregory Koukl (the website purports he's a Christian radio commentator):
http://www.str.org/free/commentaries/theology/caning.htm.

25 This info from a now-defunct website.

26 Quoted in Ric Sissons and Brian Stoddart, *Cricket and Empire*, George Allen & Unwin, Sydney, 1984, p. 21.

27 Jean Devanny, *Bird of Paradise*, Frank Johnson, Sydney, 1945, pp. 11–15.

28 *Ghostcatching: a Virtual Dance Installation*, Bill T Jones, dancer / choreographer.6 January – 13 February, 1999, Cooper Union School of Art, New York.

29 Clement Semmler (ed.), *The War Despatches of Kenneth Slessor: Official Australian Correspondent 1040-1945*, University of Queensland Press, St Lucia, Queensland, 1987, pp. 102–107.

30 Ira Gitler, notes on *Live at the Five Spot: Discovery!*, Thelonious Monk Quartet. Blue Note, 1993.

31 *Thelonious Monk with John Coltrane*, Jazzland, 0JC-039.

32 Elvis Costello, 'Brilliant Mistake', *Girls + Girls = Girls*, Demon Records, 1989.

33 Harry Mathews, *20 Lines a Day*, Dalkey Archive Press, Illinois State University, 1997, p. 15, p. 51, p. 60, p. 92.

34 Victor Shklovsky, *Mayakovsky and His Circle*, Pluto Press, London, 1974, pp. 202–203.

35 Elizabeth Bishop, 'One Art', *Complete Poems*, Chatto Poetry, London, 1991.

36 Michael Ondaatje, *Running in the Family*, Picador, London, 1985.

37 Joan Didion, *The Last Thing He Wanted*, Flamingo, London, 1997.

38 Roland Barthes, 'Style and Its Image', *The Rustle of Language*, FSG, New York, 1986.

39 Elizabeth Bishop, 'One Art', *Complete Poems*, Chatto Poetry, London, 1991.

40 Gertrude Stein, *Stanzas in Meditation: and Other Poems, 1929-1933*, Books for Libraries Press, Freeport, New York, 1969.

41 Gertrude Stein, 'Doctor Faustus Lights the Lights', *Last Operas and Plays*, Vintage Books, New York, 1975.

42 Gilles Deleuze, *Bergsonism*, Zone Books, New York, 1995.

43 Gertrude Stein, *Doctor Faustus Lights the Lights*, 1939.

44 Jean Devanny, *Bird of Paradise*, Frank Johnson, Sydney, 1945, pp. 11–15.

45 Michael Ondaatje, *Running in the Family*, Picador, London, 1985.

46 Max Brod (ed.), *The Diaries of Franz Kafka*, Schocken Books, New York [1948-49].

47 See Endnote 1.

48 See Endnote 5.

49 See Endnote 6.

50 See Endnote 8.

Bernard Cohen is the author of four previous books — *Tourism*, *The Blindman's Hat*, *Snowdome* and, most recently, *Hardly Beach Weather* — and a CD ROM, *Foreign Logics* (with David Bickerstaff). *The Blindman's Hat* won the Vogel Prize in 1996. Bernard is currently writer-in-residence at Sir John Soane's Museum (London) and University College Worcester.

John Kinsella's most recent volumes of poetry are *Visitants* and *The Hierarchy of Sheep*. His experimental novel *Genre* was published in 1996, and a collection of short fiction *Grappling Eros* in 1998. He is Professor of English at Kenyon College (USA), Adjunct Professor of Literature at Edith Cowan University, and a Fellow of Churchill College, Cambridge University.

McKenzie Wark is the author of *Virtual Geography* (Indiana University Press, 1994), *Virtual Republic* (Allen & Unwin, 1997) and *Celebrities, Culture and Cyberspace* (Pluto Press, 1999) and edits the media.culture book series for Pluto Press. He holds a PhD in Communication from Murdoch University in Western Australia and teaches writing at the State University of New York. He lives in Brooklyn with his partner Christen Clifford.

Terri-ann White has published widely, including a short story collection, *Night and Day* (1994), and a novel, *Finding Theodore and Brina* (2001). She works at the University of Western Australia, running a new cross-disciplinary research centre, and is a lifelong resident of Perth.